THE MURDER OF THEODORE BRODHEAD

John H. Abel

This is a work of historical fiction. The core of the story and the people who lived it are factual. Current-day names of places, villages, and streets have been used for clarity. Sections that appear in italics have been taken from primary documents. Some events have been dramatized and some characters are fictional. Any resemblance to any person, living or dead, is unintentional.

"The Murder of Theodore Brodhead," by John H. Abel. ISBN 978-1-949756-80-7 (softcover); 978-1-949756-81-4 (eBook).

Cover art from original oil painting by Beverly Abel.

Published 2019 by Virtualbookworm.com Publishing Inc., P.O. Box 9949, College Station, TX 77842, US.

For my wife, Beverly

CONTENTS

Chapter I: Prelude to an Unplanned Murder 1

The Courthouse--Easton, Pa. January 1868........ 3

The Robbery..12

Testimony 16

Post-Trial Proceedings 22

Easton Jail – May 1868 26

Getting Out 34

Chapter II: Wandering North to Water Gap....... 39

Walking Free... 43

Along the Way... 46

The Bachman Brothers....................................... 50

Catching a Ride.. 58

At Destiny's Doorstep 61

My Name's Ruth 63

Risk, Reward, and Opportunity 69

4th of July, 1868 - Stroudsburg........................... 72

Monday Morning Meeting................................... 75

Chapter III: Murder and Mayhem 79

Time to Move On 80

Wallace's Hardware Store – September 25, 1868
.... 84

Should be Routine 87

The Posse 93

Violent Encounter.. 94

Uncle Theodore's Been Killed 96

Apprehension and Arrest 101

Back to Jail – Stroudsburg Style 104

Chapter IV: If Before Midnight 111

The Sheriff and the Doctor 113

The Burial of Theodore Brodhead..................... 116

The Defense Team Assembles 123

Trial Day One Monday, 28 December, 1868 126

Trial Day Two 29 December, 1868.................... 133

Trial Day Three Wednesday, 30 December, 1868
.... 144

Trial Day Four Thursday, 31 December, 1868.. 148

Chapter V: "Shoot me now"...............................155

Trial Day Five Friday, January 1, 1869 157

The Verdict..159

Sentencing Saturday, January 2, 1869 162

The Governor's Mansion Harrisburg, Pa. Monday, February 1, 1869 166

The Appeal 170

Breakout..175

Billy's Dead?.. 182

Survival 184

Alone 186

The Governor's Mansion Harrisburg, Pa.
Thursday, July 1, 1869....................................... 186

Chapter VI: Let's Get This Thing Behind Us 189

Monday Morning – July 12, 1869 191

Monday Afternoon – August 9, 1869.................. 197

Tuesday, August 10, 1869................................... 202

Waiting for Death 204

The Execution of Charles Orme Wednesday,
August 11, 1869 205

The Burial of Charles Orme Friday – August 13,
1869.. 212

The Legacy of Charles Orme Saturday, August 14,
1869.. 213

Mid-January, 1900 215

Epilogue 225

Acknowledgments.. 226

Bibliography.. 228

CHAPTER I:
PRELUDE TO AN
UNPLANNED MURDER

THE COURTHOUSE--EASTON, PA.
JANUARY 1868

Although he was a judge, he exhibited little interest in the proceedings and no emotion colored his voice as he conducted them. It was a charade he maintained. It was a mask he put on every morning and took off every night. Judge Thompson was old at 60, grey since 40, and tired of the drunks, drifters, petty-thieves and dead-beats that appeared in his courtroom every Monday morning since elected to the bench in 1861.

But he was proud of his position, loved his town and cared deeply about the citizens he served. He had become increasingly concerned about the lawlessness sweeping across the country since the close of the Civil War.

In an effort to help curb that situation, he often meted out penalties considered, by some other judges, to be harsher than necessary. Among those sentenced, that opinion was unanimous.

He sat alone in his chambers this January morning, steam rising from his cup of hot tea, piles of court documents occupying every available square inch of space, but without clutter. His clerk, Abraham Horn, was a young lawyer whose fastidious habits bordered on the obsessive. He kept every detail of the judge's legal and social commitments neatly written down in a large leather binder he carried with him everywhere. Judge Thompson relied on him heavily. Today's cases had been reviewed, and decisions and comments had been neatly annotated on each document. He sipped the tea; his reading glasses fogged and his mind retreated to another time.

He thought, as he always did, of 1861. There were times when that year seemed like a lifetime ago and, at other times, he could feel it as though it were yesterday. He remembered it as a tumultuous year, a year that played in his heart and tore at his soul constantly. His cup of life held a potent mixture of joy and sorrow, and he drank from it every day.

He recalled celebrating his election to the bench with family and friends, enjoying performances at the local opera house, and late-night dinners of oysters and French wine in Easton's best hotels. In his mind's eye he pictured himself, once again, standing on the portico of the newly-constructed courthouse, high atop the Washington Street hill. There, surrounded by political dignitaries, admiring colleagues, and local well-wishers, he took the oath of office in a carefully orchestrated outdoor ceremony. His wife held the family Bible, their twenty-year-old son, Ely, stood beside her, tall and handsome. He solemnly placed his right hand on the Good Book, and in the sunlight of a warm, mid-

April afternoon, he spoke the obligatory words and became a judge.

Wanting to be first, Ely stepped forward quickly, stretched out his right hand, and with glowing admiration said, "Congratulations, Father." Smiling broadly, Judge Thompson lovingly grasped the boy's hand and replied, "Thank you, Son."

And the winds of war swept across the harbor at Charleston, South Carolina.

He was retrieved from this reverie by the entrance of his young clerk who announced in a quiet and respectful tone, "Almost time, Judge." He rose and stood by the door that led from his private chamber to the public courtroom. On this wall, by this door, he had hung a picture of his son, dressed in the uniform of the Union Army. He had not wanted the boy to enlist. He recalled overhearing him and his friends speak the phrases that had crept into the lexicon of young men in the north at this time:

'We must put down the rebellion.'

'We'll teach those traitors a lesson.'

'The Union must be preserved.'

'The enslaved will be set free.'

He understood the goodness in the boy's heart. He understood his son would take up the fight, and he understood that 1861 would never end for him.

He waited as the court-crier concluded his morning oration:

"Hear Ye - Hear Ye

All persons having business with this court

come forward now and you will be heard.

The Honorable Judge Ely Thompson presiding.

Court is now in session.

All rise."

Amid the noise of chair legs against floor boards, the creaking of old benches, old bones and throats clearing, Judge Thompson appeared, black robe neatly pressed, boots highly polished, spectacles perched mid-nose. He had more hair on his face than on top of his head. He walked to his seat with authority and an air of competence enveloped his being. In a calm, even voice he intoned, "Be seated," and the noise from 'all rise' played in reverse.

Daggers of harsh morning sunlight pierced the windows on the east wall, danced across the polished floor and collided with the glow of a wood-burning stove. Anticipation hung heavily in the air, and without looking up from the legal documents on his desk the old judge spoke a second time, "First case."

"Burglary, and burglary of one of our finest merchants," announced the crier, knowingly overstepping the legal parameters of his function. The judge winced but did not look up.

The District Attorney, Peter Haynesworth, rose. He was impeccably dressed, well-prepared, and middle everything from age weight and height, to political opinion. Judge Thompson considered him a pampered Mama's boy and didn't care at all for his effeminate mannerisms, but he knew the law, was an effective DA and popular with voters. He was one of the reasons Judge Thompson wore the mask.

The defendants, William Brooks and Charles Orme, shackled together at the waist, rose in unison. They resembled many other young men who were wandering through the American landscape in these first years after the Civil War. Drifting from town to town, unable or unwilling to find employment, they turned to crime to ward off hunger and keep themselves in liquor. They had spent the last four nights in the town jail, which had done nothing to enhance their already ragged appearance. Whatever their reasoning was, they had adopted an attitude of indifference towards the court and their own predicament. They shuffled their feet, turned to face the courtroom gallery, and while smiling nonchalantly, attempted to raise their cuffed hands as if waving to an appreciative audience.

There were about fifty people in the courtroom this cold morning and they took up about half the available seats. There were two reporters from the *Easton Sentinel*, the town's highly respected newspaper, which would soon change its name to the *Easton Express* due to a merger with another local but smaller publication. There were a handful of young men from prominent, local families who were attending Lafayette College and were considering careers in law. About a dozen others had business with the court and were patiently waiting their turn to be heard. The remainder were evenly split between those who had nothing else to do and just wanted to be entertained, or perhaps pick-up something to gossip about, and the other half, who had things to do and were putting off doing them. They were all puzzled by the posturing of these two boys, who appeared to be in their very early twenties. Their smiles were returned by no one. No one except Officer Harold Dietrich. He looked directly at them as a small, confident smile played on his clean-shaven face.

Last to rise, and not out of any disrespect, was the court-appointed defense attorney, Mr. George Meyer. He was struggling valiantly to remove his grossly overweight, poorly dressed frame from the clutch of a standard courtroom chair. Better known on the hotel circuit than the court circuit, he was of marginal ability and his plan for this morning was to plead these two indigent rascals guilty, throw them on the mercy of the court, and be at the Hotel Lafayette in time for lunch. If Judge Thompson didn't care for the district attorney, he absolutely detested the defense attorney.

But the judge always set his personal feelings aside. He had taken an oath; he had an obligation. He struggled with that every day. That was especially difficult when dealing with dishonorable young men like the two that stood before him now.

Without looking up he flatly inquired, "Which one of you is William Brooks?"

"I am," mumbled Billy, appearing bored and distracted.

That got old Judge Thompson to look up. He stared down menacingly at the rough, disheveled young man standing in front of and just below the bench.

William Brooks made a second attempt. "I am, Your Honor," straining to add an element of respect to his voice.

Judge Thompson turned his head slightly to the right, fixed his eyes on the even more pathetic figure standing to the left of Brooks, and spoke in a monotone that could have been a statement or a question, "You are Charles Orme."

"Yes, Your Honor." Charlie wasn't a particularly fast learner but he was quick to grasp the intricacies of responding to Judge Thompson.

Actually, they both well knew what was expected of them, not that they had been briefed by their attorney. This was hardly their first run-in with the law and this was not the first time they had appeared before a judge. Nor would it be the last. They were drifters; petty thieves with defiant attitudes towards authority, with no respect for the property of others.

The Judge stroked his beard thoughtfully, removed his glasses and laid them to the right of the orderly positioned papers on his desk. It wasn't just his legal mind that began considering the situation confronting the court this morning. He had a feeling about these two, a sixth sense. Intuition told him something more ominous was brewing under the surface with this pair. But fair and impartial he would be; he always was. He replaced his glasses and picked up the written report of Patrolman Dietrich, the arresting officer. He returned his gaze to the shackled young men and spoke:

"You have both been charged with burglary, but your attorney has argued, not very convincingly, that the charge should be reduced to attempted burglary since you were not successful in your endeavors."

Judge Thompson, taking a measure of satisfaction in his little discourse, continued.

"It does not appear to me that either of you have ever been successful at anything worthwhile. Is that correct?"

Staring at the floor, Billy and Charlie mumbled, "Yes Your Honor," almost in unison, which brought forth an admonition from the judge to look up and speak up when answering. And the judge wasn't done. "I want to know more about this, burglary, attempted burglary," and directed his next command at the bailiff saying, "Get Patrolman Dietrich up here." A little emotion crept into the judge's tone.

The bailiff formally called for the patrolman and young Harold Dietrich came forward, stood rigidly alongside the prosecutor's table, and was duly sworn.

Known as Harry to his friends, young Mr. Dietrich was a dedicated patrolman. He had grown up in Easton, joined the Union Army in '64, and was proud to have marched across Georgia and into the Carolinas with General William Tecumseh Sherman. He took to the discipline and regimentation of army life, so he fit right into a job with the police force which consisted of a chief, Herman Bachman, and a sergeant who worked during the day, and four patrolmen who worked evenings covering their assigned sections of the town, which had been divided into four "beats."

The charade of impartiality and the mask of objectivity was always projected by the judge, but everyone knew that Judge Thompson had a special liking for Harry Dietrich. The judge's son was only four years older than Harry and the judge could recall many a summer afternoon when, as children, the boys played together in the shallow water where the Lehigh and Delaware Rivers converge. He saw them now, in his mind's eye, Ely throwing a ball to young Harry, encouraging him to catch it and throw it back quickly and accurately.

Ely was like an older brother to Harry. He stepped in when older boys from the south-side tried to pick on Harry, teasing him because of his small size, or when their horseplay turned too rough. Ely could tell when Harry felt threatened; that's when he would come to his aid. Ely wasn't a fighter, but he was tall for his age and everyone knew his father was an attorney. The rough boys weren't afraid of Ely but, in their minds, he represented money and power. So, they dispersed to the back streets and the alleys when he stepped onto the scene.

The judge remembered the boys on a snowy, wintry night, trudging up Northampton Street and sledding down the steep grade, Ely with a new sled and Harry with a piece of box covered with animal hide. He saw Ely sharing the sled, taking the old piece of box for himself every other ride down the hill.

These were the memories he clung to when he envisioned his son lying in a field, bleeding to death from a bullet in his chest, at the Battle of Bull Run in July, 1861. Seven years had passed and still there was no relief from the pain. He looked up at Patrolman Dietrich and remembered him as a teenage boy crying bitterly by Ely's coffin.

"Good morning, Officer Dietrich." The judge's tone was even and business-like as he snapped himself back to the reality of the day.

"Good morning, Your Honor." Harry understood what was expected of him and what was not.

THE ROBBERY

Patrolman Dietrich knew about half the story and he would do a good job relating the details of the crime, as he knew them, when asked to do so by Judge Thompson. The only people in the courtroom that knew the whole story were, of course, the two boys who were on trial.

They knew how they had closely monitored Walter Bishop's clock shop on the town square for two weeks, how they devised a plan to gain entry to the premises through a seldom used weakly secured door in the rear of the building. They had paid special attention to the amount of wagon, buggy and pedestrian traffic that used the alley behind the store and noted that, for some unknown reason, no one ever travelled the unlit back street on a Thursday night. They were precariously low on cash with only a few items remaining, some socks, a pair of gloves and one good belt, to sell or barter. They had to pull-off a robbery soon or be reduced to hiring on as day-laborers for some local business.

Determined to avoid working for wages, a function they both hated and always failed at, they prepared for their clandestine, nocturnal caper.

"That's enough, no more whiskey," Brooks admonished Orme, "We need clear heads tonight."

Charles Orme grunted in agreement, placed the bottle back on the table and rammed the cork into the neck.

"Is it time?" Orme was anxious to do the job and get back to his bottle.

"Yeah, late enough, dark enough, don't see no moon. Time for us to replenish our treasury," said Brooks as he blew out the single candle that dimly lit their dingy room on the third floor of the boarding house they had been occupying for the past month.

"Let's go." Billy's tone masked his nervousness.

They carefully descended the rickety, wooden stairs that clung precariously to the clapboard siding of Peter Nungesser's hotel on Green Street, just 100 feet from the edge of the Delaware River, the boundary between Pennsylvania and New Jersey. They paused in the dark, cluttered alley while their eyes adjusted to the blackness. They would need to pick their way around the broken, discarded flotsam of a town rapidly outgrowing itself.

William spoke in a hushed tone, "Charlie, listen. We go in, we take the best stuff we see, we get out. Quick and quiet, ten, maybe fifteen minutes."

"How the hell will I know what to take? I can't see in the dark." Desperation filled Charlie's whispered words.

"It'll be alright," Billy said reassuringly. "Remember that old man, that old lamplighter man? There was a good reason I watched him. Every night, around 10:30, he lights the street lamp, right in front of the store. That'll give us just enough light. You gotta keep yourself under control, alright?"

"Right," Charlie whispered. Charlie always agreed with Billy. Charlie took orders from Billy because Charlie believed Billy was smarter. Even though Charlie stood half a foot taller, outweighed Billy by fifty pounds and at 24 was three years older, it was

14

Billy who planned the robberies and, Charlie figured, since they'd only been caught and thrown in jail twice before, Billy was doing a good job as the leader.

"Long before the sun comes up, we'll be riding the ferry to the other side of that river, safe and sound in New Jersey, where we can explore some new business opportunities and meet some new girls." Billy smiled as he explained.

"Hey, is that why you give that old ferryman a bottle of our good hard cider, so as he'll take us across?" Charlie asked, sounding proud of himself for having figured something out.

"Sure is. He's gonna meet us at the landing right at four o'clock. That's just about four hours from now. He said if we're late he won't wait. Scared of getting caught. I promised him another bottle after he gets us across the river. He doesn't know anything and all he cares about is that bottle of cider. Even if he did say something, who's gonna believe an old drunk like him? I don't think people pay any attention to him anyhow."

"You sure are something, Billy." Charlie really did trust Billy with his welfare.

"Now, no more talking. You gotta keep your mouth shut till we finish this job and get back to the hotel. Then we pack up a couple things and we make it on down to the landing and we get on the other side of that river."

Silently they began navigating their way through the dark, narrow alley. Nearby, a dog barked, angrily announcing their passing, and William Brooks made a mental note to return by a different route. They arrived at the shop's back door just as the town clock tolled midnight. Sporadic moonlight filtered through the clouds, offering just enough candlepower for Billy to locate and silently slide the heavy dead-bolt out of its housing. He pulled gently on the door, opening it only an inch or two, listening for creaks and squeaks from the old rusty hinges that would betray his criminal activity. He continued opening the old back-door slowly, just a little at a time. The space between the edge of the door and the worm-eaten frame gradually enlarged to two feet. Billy Brooks knew he would need another foot. He mentally cursed his overweight partner-in-crime for making this extra effort necessary. Billy did, at times, call Charlie a fat ass. Sometimes he was just teasing and sometimes he was serious but all the time he knew Charles Orme didn't like being called a fat ass.

TESTIMONY

"Now, Patrolman Dietrich," Judge Thompson said, "I want you to tell the court, in your own words, the details of this burglary or attempted burglary, as you witnessed it, at the business of Mr. Walter Bishop, on the night of," glancing down then right back up, the Judge continued, "Thursday, January 9, 1868. Go ahead son, and speak up."

District Attorney Haynesworth was delighted Judge Thompson had taken over the proceedings.

He had more important things on his mind than these two second- rate thieves. Even though they had entered guilty pleas, he would make sure his friends at the newspaper wrote up a convincing story about him getting a conviction and of his ongoing dedication to law and order. To make himself look good, he had decided he would speak up if Judge Thompson imposed a jail sentence of less than 120 days, but, he was pretty sure that wasn't going to be necessary. He smiled to himself, satisfied that his career in law and politics was progressing nicely.

"Very well, Your Honor." Young Harry spoke calmly, his voice filling the courtroom with integrity. "I climbed the outdoor stairs at Mrs. Rinker's School for Girls and positioned myself on the second-floor balcony. As you know, that establishment, Mrs. Rinker's, is at the entrance to Orr's Alley.

The judge nodded in agreement while an assortment of hushed sounds rippled outward from the center of the courtroom, where Harry's friends, fellow patrolmen, and the newsmen were seated. Almost everyone knew that Mrs. Rinker ran a whorehouse out of her large Victorian home in Orr's Alley and a few knew that Thursday night was Harry's night to visit. People refrained from using the alley on Thursday night. Everybody loved Harry. Harry kept everybody safe all the time, and everybody allowed Harry some private time on Thursday nights. Except for a little extra color in his cheeks, Harry continued his testimony unabated and unembarrassed.

"Mrs. Rinker had just offered me a cup of coffee, which I declined, and when she went back inside I saw some movement in the shadows below me, at the back door of Bishop's Clock Shop. It's only about one hundred feet to the store, so I could make out two men entering the premises, and it was just after midnight because I had heard the church bell ring twelve times. I drew my revolver and started down the stairs, being careful not to make any noise. I came up to the rear of the building and saw they had left the door open and I could see their silhouettes by the light of the nearby street lamp. Old man Auchenbach, I mean Mr. Auchenbach, well, his dog was carrying on something terrible and I was afraid these boys wouldn't be able to hear my commands."

Judge Thompson slid to the edge of his chair, removed his glasses and spoke to Harry in a fatherly tone, "Let's move it along , Officer."

"Yes, Your Honor." And Harry continued. "I called out pretty loud, 'Easton Police, hands up and come out.' I could tell, even in the dim light that they didn't have any weapons drawn, but I kept my revolver pointed directly at them anyway. I blew three short blasts on my whistle, loud as I could, that's the signal for other patrolmen to come fast and render assistance. Jimmy and Bobby Kilpatrick, two other patrolmen, got there just as these two defendants were coming out with their hands over their heads. At this point they had three revolvers aimed at them so they offered no resistance. They were cuffed and searched and we took a knife from each of them and one .44 caliber pistol from William Brooks. They didn't have any store merchandise on them. We all marched off to the jail, going around the long way so as we didn't have to put up with that dog, and they've been in jail since then. That's about it, Your Honor."

"If I may Your Honor," the defense attorney called out as he again struggled to gain a vertical position.

"What is it, Attorney Meyer?" The judge was back to speaking in his unemotional tone.

"May I inquire as to why Patrolman Dietrich was standing on Mrs. Rinker's balcony at that hour of the night?"

"You may," the judge pronounced. "I was curious about that myself."

Close friends and a few other patrolmen looked anxiously at Harry. They weren't concerned only for him. Young Harry wasn't the only man on the police force who felt it his duty to check on the welfare of Mrs. Rinker and her staff from time to time. Some officers held their breath, knowing they would live or die by what Officer Dietrich told the court.

"Do you understand the question, Patrolman Dietrich?" asked Judge Thompson.

"I do Your Honor, and I'm glad I have been asked to explain that because it allows me the opportunity to introduce to the court not only the source of my information, and recognize him for his community service, but I'll also show evidence regarding the defendants' intent to flee our jurisdiction after committing the crime."

The collective sigh of relief from a large portion of the male contingent in the courtroom resembled the sound of air escaping a balloon.

"Your Honor, these poor unfortunate young men have already agreed to...." and that's as far as Attorney Meyer got before Judge Thompson told him to sit down and be quiet

"Continue Patrolman Dietrich." The judge was running low on patience.

Harry was comfortable speaking in court; in fact, he kind of enjoyed it, so he slowed the pace of his delivery. Knowing he was listened to with some interest, he lowered the volume of his voice, and on he went: "I had been informed of the strong possibility of a robbery occurring in that alley late on Thursday night. The exact time and location of the crime could not be known for certain, but I was given enough information to position myself in the right place at the right time. And that information came to me from one of the town's ferrymen, Mr. Jacob Abel. The police department owes him a debt of gratitude for his service. Furthermore, as proof of their intention to flee after the robbery, Jacob had been given a bottle of hard cider as payment to take these two across river at four o'clock in the morning. And here, Your Honor, is the bottle that Jacob was given." Patrolman Dietrich reached behind the seat of the District Attorney and held up a glass bottle complete with a cork protruding from its neck.

"I'm going to assume that empty bottle had something in it when it was given to ferryman Abel," noted the defense attorney, and all those in the courtroom broke out in laughter, all those except the judge and the defendants.

Judge Thompson gaveled the courtroom back to order. Everyone knew the judge was done listening, had come to a conclusion, and was ready to render his verdict.

"In light of the evidence that's been presented before the court this morning, it is the court's opinion that the crime of attempted burglary has been committed by the two defendants and that they should be housed in the jail of the city of Easton for a period of ninety days. This court also imposes an additional thirty days incarceration for attempting to bribe a public official."

Defense Attorney Meyer, surprised by the sound of his own voice and his quick escape from the chair, called out, "Pardon me, Your Honor, when did ferryman Abel become a public official?"

"Last Thursday," and the judge banged the gavel, again quieting the snickering and laughing that arose from the gallery. He turned his head and spoke directly to the bailiff. "Have these two removed from my courtroom and taken to the jail and if there's any trouble while they're in jail, I want to know about it immediately." His next targets were Brooks and Orme themselves and he spoke to them in an almost challenging tone, "You'll be wise to obey the rules of our jail for the next four months because if any report of behavior other than strict compliance reaches me, you'll be spending even more time behind bars here in our fair city. And speaking of our fair city, I'm instructing you both, right now, that at the end of this four month sentence, you two high-tail it out of Easton and you stay out of Easton. I'll be instructing the Chief of Police to arrest and detain both of you if he ever sees either of you again. Understood?"

"Yes, Your Honor." Defeat registered in their tone and demeanor for the first time. It was as if Brooks and Orme just realized that spring was a long way off.

"That's enough for this morning." Judge Thompson spoke in an even voice, indicating that he had returned to the emotionless arbiter of liberty and justice.

As he rose, he struck the gavel for the final time of the morning session and the court-crier sang out, "All rise, court is in recess until two o'clock."

POST-TRIAL PROCEEDINGS

Judge Thompson closed the door to his office and stood for a moment, silently contemplating the case just concluded. He stared at the picture of Ely, the soldier, the warrior, the fallen son. Brooks and

Orme would go free in the spring but his boy would remain in the grave.

In the courtroom, there was the usual milling about after the close of the morning session. Some discussed the case just concluded, others complained about having to wait to be heard until the afternoon session. Almost all were making some kind of lunch plans, and of course, the lawyers were shaking hands and exchanging the standard congratulatory or sympathetic remarks.

James and Robert Kilpatrick, the two patrolmen who had come to assist in the Thursday night arrest, walked up to Harry and shook his hand, complimenting him on his fine testimony, which was code for not divulging the details of Mrs. Rinker's School for Girls. The three young men smiled knowingly at each other. There was a bond between them. As boys they had not been friends. The Kilpatrick brothers hailed from the south-side and ran with the boys that had sometimes picked on Harry until Ely stepped in. They were boys then. Now, they were young men and all that was past; forgotten, forgiven. Jimmy and Bobby were a little older than Harry and had gone off to war on the same train with Ely Thompson, but family connections and social status soon separated them. Ely was assigned to a unit that did not anticipate engaging in any real combat, while Jimmy and Bobby ended up with the 116th Pennsylvania Regiment. The 116th Pennsylvania was melded into the 63rd, the 69th, the 88th New York and the 28th Massachusetts, the famous Irish Brigade. They fought at Antietam, Fredericksburg, Chancellorsville and Gettysburg. They suffered more casualties than any other brigade, lost two men in combat for every one man lost to disease - the opposite of the ratio for the Union Army as a whole.

Abraham Horn, Judge Thompson's loyal and attentive law clerk, tapped on the heavy oak door that led to the judge's private chambers. He lifted the latch and pushed the door open just enough to see the judge, who was still standing, silent and stooped, staring at the portrait of his son in uniform.

Young Abraham instinctively understood the judge would be melancholy the rest of the day. He knew the judge would not speak much or show much emotion. He would retreat to a private place, deep inside himself, where people couldn't see the pain and bitterness still in his broken heart.

"I have your lunch tray ready judge; shall I bring it in?" Abraham asked quietly.

"Yes," the judge replied, turning his head from Ely's picture to his clerk.

Before leaving the house that morning he had asked his wife, Elizabeth, if she would join him for lunch at Youell's Oyster House, a small establishment located halfway between the courthouse and their home. She declined, citing the extreme cold as her reason for not wanting to venture out. She quickly prepared a lunch for him to take, deftly cutting two slices of recently baked rye bread upon which she placed a generous portion of roast chicken, left over from the night before. She ladled some bean soup into a tin he sometimes carried to the courthouse.

"Don't forget to bring the tin home tonight," smiling as she reminded him.

"I always bring the tin home, except when I forget," smiling at her and his response.

She was a petite woman, always properly dressed, grey hair piled on top of her head. She was pleasant and polite, active in the library guild and the Lutheran Church. The years had been kind to her; she did not appear to be 59 years old. She had weathered the storm of their son's death better than the judge had, drawing on her religious beliefs to sustain her during that devastating time and in the years following. She was the pillar the judge leaned on.

He ate his lunch alone, looking over some court papers relating to the afternoon session, but he could not focus. His thoughts were still on the morning case. He looked up from the paperwork and put down his cup of soup. His mind tumbled the names over and over.

"Brooks and Orme" .... "Brooks and Orme".......... Wherever they ended up, there'd be trouble. The premonition lingered.

EASTON JAIL – MAY 1868

They had been in jail elsewhere, but this Easton jail was different. They were not pushed and punched or spoken to in the usual harsh and degrading tones. No effort was made to belittle them for their past transgressions. Their stint had not been a cake-walk, but they were not dehumanized by their jailers either. They were expected to maintain a high level of personal hygiene. They were allowed to use the outhouse whenever necessary, and every Saturday they were allowed a hot bath in a room set aside for that purpose. Once a month, one of the town barbers, who also functioned as a dentist, came by the jail and provided haircuts and shaves and extracted teeth when asked to do so. There were infractions of the jail house rules, and they both were punished on more than one occasion. When punishment was meted out it was usually for something like not keeping their bunks and blankets neat or not cleaning properly when assigned to housekeeping duty. A reduction in the quantity of food served (although they did receive three meals every day), or a curtailment in the privilege of sitting in the enclosed outdoor courtyard was about the extent of their punishment. Physical violence was never used, nor was it even threatened. Such treatment seemed unusual to William Brooks though it had greater impact on Charles Orme who, from time to time, noted the lack of corporal punishment.

Billy and Charlie were not the only prisoners occupying a cell at the town jail in the winter and spring of 1868. They had seen some bloody brawls between the guards and the inmates, but never did the jailers retaliate except to subdue and restrain. Charles seemed to recognize the goodness in this, and in his heart that made him feel something, but 'what' he could not say; he had no words for goodness, kindness, fairness. Those sentiments were unfamiliar to him.

Billy was stretched out on his bunk, staring up at the ceiling, totally absorbed in planning for their release, just two weeks away. So complete was his concentration that he did not see nor hear the guard approaching until he stood right outside the cell.

"Up Mr. Brooks, up off the bunk." It was Joshua Kern, the day guard. He was strict and nothing went unnoticed on his watch, but he never meted out any punishment. He spoke an order to correct a situation and that was the end of it. In his mid-twenties, he was the youngest of the three guards that worked at the jail - he always worked during the day. He arrived at the jail each morning before sunrise; by mid-afternoon was gone till next morning.

William Brooks swung his feet out over the straw-filled mattress and pushed himself into a standing position. "Whatever you say, Mr. Boss Man." Billy liked to maintain a sense of humor whenever he was in jail.

Young Joshua checked the lock on the cell that held Brooks and Orme, then walked down the narrow hallway, checking locks and the condition of other men held in cells that morning. He found nothing to be concerned about or that needed reporting, so he returned to the small room in the front of jail where the warden sat at his desk, and announced "all secure, Warden."

Ezra Bachman was the warden and no one could remember a time when he wasn't the warden. He was the brother of the Chief of Police, Herman Bachman, and together they were responsible for law and order in the city; they answered to no one other than the mayor.

Ezra, a large man in his mid-fifties, was never without a cigar in his mouth, although it was not always lit. He gave Joshua a nod and went back to reading the police reports sent to the jail each morning by his brother, the Chief. He was not the kind of man that developed a relationship with his subordinates, but he rarely found fault with them and stayed out of their way as they did their jobs. He was a man of few words, but respected by those who worked for him.

In addition to the warden's desk there was a gun cabinet, which held rifles, pistols and ammo, a wood burning stove, a church pew, a spittoon, an old wooden cabinet used for filing the reports and documents necessary to running a jail, and a safe which housed the items taken from prisoners upon their incarceration.

In the far corner of the room, by the door that led out to an enclosed yard, sat Bones, a large black dog of unknown ancestry. Bones didn't belong to anyone in particular, and he didn't serve any real purpose, but one time he barked during an escape attempt and that earned him two meals a day and a blanket in the corner. Everybody was happy with the arrangement, especially Bones, who spent most of the day sleeping.

There was a rhythm to life and work at the town's jail that nobody was more in tune with than Bones. During the morning the warden read his reports and smoked his cigars and Joshua checked on the condition of the prisoners and reported his findings, or lack of them, to the warden. There was activity during the afternoon when prisoners were released back into society, a function handled by the warden with assistance from Joshua and the second shift jailer, a young man named Luke Werkheiser.

Joshua wasn't sure how he felt about Luke. They'd been working together for three months and Joshua still didn't know anything about him. Luke wasn't from Easton and word was he had an uncle on the town council who used his influence to secure the position at the jail for him. No one knew where he came from or what he had done before arriving in Easton. He offered no information about himself and did not respond to any of Joshua's attempts to make conversation. Although Joshua had enlisted in the Union Army late in the war and had seen no combat, he had a feeling Luke had not served at all. Luke was not overly ambitious nor did he give any indication of wanting to learn and advance himself, unlike Joshua, who saw himself as warden someday or maybe even Chief of Police. On top of all that, Bones didn't like him.

As afternoons darkened into evenings, Thomas Spangler arrived at the jail for his shift. A little older than Joshua and Luke, he was an able young man who was outgoing and always cheerful. He was alone on the night shift which could be either the easiest or the most difficult time on duty. He had broad shoulders, a barrel chest, stood well over six feet tall and was capable of handling any situation that came up, which was important, because the night shift was the time when the police brought the drunks and the brawlers into the lock-up. Although Thomas never spoke of it, it was rumored he had stood and fought, turning back the onslaught of General Pickett's gallant charge on the last day at Gettysburg. On top of all that, Bones liked him. Thomas brought the dog scraps, so Bones stayed near Thomas as he completed his nightly 'walk-about' around the perimeter of the jail.

Charles Orme rested his elbows on the wooden sill of the small, barred window on the back wall of the cell he and William Brooks had occupied since January. He had looked out from here many times, contemplating the visual changes in the landscape. Just a few months ago the river had been frozen over. Today it flowed unimpeded on its way to Philadelphia, the Delaware Bay, and the Atlantic Ocean. Trees, once barren, were now touched with the promising green of spring. His face turned calm and his eyes stared far away, lost in a day-dream of better times.

Billy sauntered over to him. "Don't be getting all soft on me now fat ass. Just two weeks and we'll be walking free. Free men going where we please."

"It wasn't that bad, was it?" Charlie asked.

"I guess not." Billy answered.

"They give us decent grub, and we had a warm place to sleep." Charlie stated.

"Jesus, I do say. Maybe we should get us thrown in jail every winter. Would you like that?" Billy was egging Charlie on now.

"They treated us fair. It was nice on days when them church ladies come. Bringing us cookies and bread and shit they made. There was that one girl. She was pretty. She give me a Bible to read and she smiled at me. I think she liked me. I do." Charlie turned his gaze back to the window and the river just beyond.

Billy laughed out loud. "Who the hell would like a fat old mule like you, 'cept maybe another fat old mule?"

"Yeah, well, I didn't see none of 'em smiling at you." It was rare for Charlie to challenge Billy, and he quickly changed his tone. " 'Cept the work. I didn't like all that work we had to do. Cutting them weeds and brush and lugging it all uphill to that big old wagon last week. And painting this damn jail inside and out. Bad enough I got to be in it."

Without really understanding, Billy thought it was good for Charlie to talk and get it off his chest, about having spent four months in jail, so he let him ramble on, pretending not only to listen but be interested in what Charlie was saying.

"But that railroad thing," Charlie continued, "that was shit."

In February of 1868, a blizzard came through the area, and snow and drifts stopped all transportation. Nothing was moving and the citizens of Easton and the surrounding area were hard pressed for food and fuel for heat. The basic necessities of life were cut off; everyone suffered.

The Mayor put out a call for volunteers to clear roads and any pathways so people could get food, and medical attention should an emergency come up. The turnout was good. Policemen and firemen were first to respond, followed by the churches and the civic organizations including a strong showing by the members of the Grand Army of the Republic, a fraternal organization composed of veterans of the Union Army.

The throng of volunteers huddled together in the town square, awaiting orders and shielding themselves from the storm's fury. They were no match for the volume of snow delivered by the mid-February blizzard. Chief Bachman sought out Patrolman Dietrich, and shouting loudly to be heard over the howling wind, yelled in his ear, "Go find my brother. Tell him to pick some prisoners he could trust with a shoveling detail. We're going to need men to clean out tracks so trains can get through."

Brooks and Orme were among the five selected for this detail. The prisoners boarded a wagon, and at a spot about two miles south of town they were ordered out of the wagon and instructed to stand in line. Each man was issued a pair of heavy-duty railroad work gloves and a shovel. Instructions were simple and to the point: "Clear the tracks and you'll receive extra rations at breakfast; run, and you'll be shot."

A guard stood on each side of the tracks, a lantern in one hand, a rifle in the other. The prisoners began shoveling.

By morning, the wind had subsided and the snow had dwindled down to light flurries. Exhausted, cold and hungry, the prisoners were shepherded back into the wagon; a pair of mules, also exhausted, cold and hungry began stepping through three feet of snow, pulling the worn-out band of shovelers and guards back to town.

Good to their word, there was extra bacon and biscuits, and even sugar for the strong black coffee that morning.

"I seem to recall you ate pretty good that morning," Billy teased.

Charlie continued staring out at the river.

GETTING OUT

Over the past four months, Billy and Charlie had seen a fair number of other prisoners released, so they were familiar with the procedure that would set them free. They had learned the most important lessons of getting out of the Easton jail. Act respectful; don't ask questions; leave quietly. They considered themselves well prepared for their release, so on Monday, May 11, they woke and rose with the sun and the sound of birds ushering in a spring day and a new start. They set themselves to their regular duties of folding blankets, drawing pails of water from the pump in the middle of the jail yard, and sweeping out their cell and down the hall, all under the watchful eye of the morning guard, Joshua. They ambled back to their cell where Joshua closed and locked their cell door. Some elements of this last day would very much resemble the first day.

"So, what do you think Mr. Kern? How soon do we go?" Excitement filled Billy's voice as he anticipated their imminent release.

He and Charlie had grown used to addressing the guards as "Mr." It was a professional law enforcement courtesy used by everyone. It was also a discipline that maintained the gap between jailer and prisoner. Even the warden, who was always addressed as "Warden," called the guards "Mr."

"You've been here long enough to know how it works. Mid-afternoon, when Mr. Werkheiser arrives for his shift, you'll be sent on your way." Joshua was perfunctory in his response. He kept prisoners at arm's length and built no rapport with any of them. Off duty, surrounded by friends, he was an outgoing, cheerful young man.

"Do you think?", was all Billy managed before Joshua's flat response of, "That's enough for now, Mr. Brooks," cut his question short.

Returning to the office section of the jail, Joshua completed his morning reports and put them on the warden's desk. Bones got up from his corner blanket, walked out the back door and peed in the blooming daffodils.

To the surprise of no one, Luke Werkheiser, second shift jailer, was late to arrive for his shift. Warden Bachman was at his wit's end with this tardiness, and even more aggravated that he couldn't address the situation, due to the meddling of some member of the town council. He made a mental note to talk again to his brother, the chief of police, about this. The warden had a good reason for wanting Brooks and Orme released in the early part of the afternoon rather than later. He wanted as many miles as possible between them and the town of Easton before nightfall. The more daylight they had, the further they could walk. Judge Thompson wasn't alone in feeling these two were capable of much worse than stealing.

Upon entering the jail, Luke offered a half-hearted greeting to the warden and Joshua. He made no attempt at an apology or excuse for being late. Joshua acknowledged him with a nod, but the warden didn't bother looking up from his paperwork. Bones opened his eyes, saw Luke had arrived, and went back to sleep.

"Alright, let's have 'em." The warden's command was understood, and Joshua, followed by Luke, proceeded down the hall to the cell that held Brooks and Orme.

"Come to the door," Joshua stated in an even voice. Joshua and Luke had positioned themselves in front of the cell that had been the residence of Billy and Charlie for the past four months. Joshua turned the key in the lock and swung the door open. Charlie and Billy stepped out into the hall and all four of them proceeded toward the warden's desk, Luke leading the way, followed by Billy, then Charlie, then Joshua. They anticipated no trouble; it wouldn't make any sense to break and run now; the thieves were on their way to freedom.

They stood in front of the warden in the same order while Warden Bachman, seated in his well-cushioned chair, shuffled through their release papers for what seemed, to Billy and Charlie, like an eternity. Two small canvas bags, one labeled William Brooks, the other, Charles Orme, rested in the center of his desk. Finally, he raised head, peered out over his rimless spectacles, and through a cloud of cigar smoke addressed them in a professional, business-like way.

"We've had no serious trouble with you two, so you'll be on your way in a couple minutes. These bags contain your belongings. Things you had when you were brought here. Open them now and inspect the contents. If you feel you've been cheated out of anything, speak up."

They each opened their bag and emptied the sparse contents on the warden's desk. A small pocket knife and some coins, along with a compass, were the worldly possessions of Charles Orme.

A larger pocket knife, a few coins, a button, and a pair of shoelaces were the items contained in the bag marked 'William Brooks.'

Much to the surprise of both boys, a dollar bill had been placed in each bag and they stared at the warden with questioning expressions.

"You worked for the Pennsylvania Railroad for ten hours. That's your pay." The warden's tone was matter-of-fact. Everyone knew he did not approve of paying prisoners for any work they did, anywhere, for anyone. But eastern Pennsylvania was learning, as was the rest of the United States, that you did what the railroads wanted done. Bones opened his eyes and watched the warden move across the room, open the safe and remove a .44 caliber Colt revolver. He lumbered back to his chair and grunted as he repositioned himself behind the desk.

"This is your property. I never want to see it, or either of you, again. If I do, there'll be hell to pay," and he handed the gun, butt-end first, to Billy

Brooks, who could hardly believe his good fortune. A dollar for shoveling snow and his prized Colt revolver, model 1860, back in his possession.

His throat was dry, his hand trembled slightly, and as he took the gun from the warden he managed a whispered "Thank you."

"That's all. Good luck to you both," and Warden Ezra Bachman was done with Billy Brooks and Charlie Orme, for now.

They passed through the front door of the jail with Joshua and Luke behind them and stood in the yard on the edge of the dusty road that ran along the river. It was late afternoon and a gentle breeze came up off the river, carrying a hint of honeysuckle in its warm embrace. The four men stopped and awkwardly looked at each other, wondering what to say or if anything at all should be said. Billy broke the silence. "I was thinking due north." He wasn't conferring with his partner, he was asking Joshua. Joshua turned and faced north, then spoke directly to Billy. "Small town up that way. Stroudsburg. Three, maybe four-day walk. Old boys up there don't take to stealin'."

It was a kindly warning to Brooks and Orme, but they both ignored it.

CHAPTER II:
WANDERING NORTH
TO WATER GAP

WALKING FREE

The small dusty road meandered out in front of them in a northerly direction and, for the most part, ran parallel to the southerly flowing Delaware River. Billy decided he and Charlie would leave the city of Easton by this route.

They began their exodus at a leisurely pace, sometimes talking and bantering, other times walking in silence, each man lost in the solitude of his own thoughts.

Mid-spring vegetation bordered each side of the narrow road and a thin green strip battled for survival in the middle, a haven for snakes and biting insects. Groundhogs, alerted to their approach, stood on hind legs, peeked at them over lush clover, then darted to the safety of their burrows.

"I used to shoot them when I was a boy. My Ma would cook 'em up and we ate them with potatoes. They was a good meal as I recall." Charlie's voice was tinged with the tone of a young man remembering boyhood and happier times. Billy, having no similar recollections, offered no response. Billy would not have wasted a bullet on a groundhog, but Charlie's story reminded him that he couldn't shoot the varmint, even if he wanted to.

"Still pisses me off, them people not returning my cartridges. Think I had seven of 'em." Billy wasn't actually talking to Charlie, he was just talking and Charlie happened to be within earshot.

Charlie responded anyway, "Yeah, well, you had your chance. That old warden said to speak up if you felt you was cheated out of anything."

Billy had to laugh, "You're right, Charlie. Just can't figure why that old bastard wouldn't give bullets to a fine, upstanding citizen like myself."

Billy was determined to replace the cartridges one way or another, and he wanted to obtain a pistol for Charlie as well.

Each day grew a little longer, a little warmer, and a little more tiring. They noticed the changes in the terrain. The hills became steeper, the roadway rockier. Trees, fully flowered at the beginning of their journey, now held just miniature leaves. The air was so laden with pollen that their eyes watered and they sometimes fell into fits of coughing.

Billy, always the instigator, would sometimes challenge Charlie to games of physical ability. These duals helped pass the time and also served to cement Billy's position as leader of the duo. Billy had a knack for coming up with things to do; things he knew he could do better than Charlie.

"I'll bet I can hit that tree with a stone more times than you can." Billy said.

"What tree?" asked Charlie.

"That tree, right there," Billy said, pointing, "the one with the hole half-way up the trunk."

They each selected an assortment of five small stones, and sure enough, Billy outscored Charlie, three to one.
A few miles later it was a competition to see who could throw a stone the greatest distance. Billy's stone reached the river and entered the water with a loud, splashing sound. Charlie's stone fell short and buried itself in the mud of the river bank.

The 'I'll bet you' phrase was nothing more than an expression Billy used to start an endeavor. Neither of them had anything of value to bet with, but Billy liked the games; he liked beating Charlie, and of course, Billy always had a plan.

"I'll bet you I can run over there, to that maple tree, jump up, and come down with a handful of them little leaves, right off that first branch. I'll even bet you that railroad dollar you got tucked away in your boot." No sooner had Billy said that when he realized he had overstepped his leadership role. He quickly tried to back-track. "Never mind, you're too fat for jumping anyway."

Somewhat annoyed and just a little suspicious, Charlie replied, "Yeah, you're right. I'm too fat, and I'm too hungry for jumping. And I didn't want nobody to see me put that dollar in my boot. I'm saving that dollar for when we get somewhere, anywhere, then I'm buying myself a decent meal."

ALONG THE WAY

Somewhere was, indeed, out there, over the horizon. Wide spots in the road like Sandt's Eddy and tiny villages like Martin's Creek and Stone Church lay just beyond. The road became wider, more heavily used, and cut its way through little towns like Mt. Bethel and Portland. All of this was unknown and unfamiliar to William Brooks and Charles Orme.

Their luck had held for the first week. Warm temperatures, clear skies and, most importantly, farm families had taken them in each night. In exchange for some work around the properties, they were fed and given a place to sleep, usually in the hayloft of the barn. On each of the three farms they stopped at they were asked about their wartime service.

They encountered weeping mothers, still bitter fathers, and at the last farm, a young man, a veteran, about their own age, with no legs. The boy was cheerful and worked at different jobs on the farm. He could split firewood, milk cows, and work in the vegetable patch. His wounds didn't slow him down very much and the rest of the family, two younger sisters, an older brother, and his mother and father, didn't treat him any differently than if he had come home intact. Except for their time in the Easton jail, where they knew two of the three young jailers had served in the Union Army, by the stories they had heard, this contact with a crippled veteran was a new experience. Billy was apprehensive from the moment he laid eyes on the legless young man.

Billy and Charlie had put together, over the past three years, a selection of stories about their service in the Union Army. They didn't make themselves out to be heroes, nor did they admit to being the draft-dodgers that they actually were. The tales were short summations of an enlistment that never happened, but they worked on grieving wives and mothers and fathers and brothers. They had worked out the details of these falsehoods for several reasons. First, they were usually asked about their wartime service, so being prepared was necessary, and secondly, a good story could yield some extra food, a comfortable place to spend the night, and on the luckiest of occasions, some whiskey.

But this legless person was different. When he addressed Billy and Charlie he called them Mr. Brooks and Mr. Orme. He spoke as an educated man would speak so Billy reasoned he had probably been an officer. As such he would be familiar with the way an army is structured. He would know about Companies, Regiments and Brigades, Divisions and Corps. Although only in his company during and briefly after the evening meal, he made Billy uneasy. When he spoke he looked directly into the eyes of the person he was addressing.

Billy decided, if it became necessary, he would get as close to a prepared story as he could and hope no glaring errors in his tale would reveal the true nature of their contact with the Union Army during the last few months of the War. He had some concern that Charlie might butt-in and try to correct him on parts of the story, but Charlie was busy keeping his mouth full of ham and potatoes and the put-up green beans that every farmhouse kitchen held in reserve.

After saying 'Grace,' minimum conversation went round the dinner table. Everyone was hungry and ate quickly and as the meal drew to a close the mother spoke. "Please clear the table girls. Does anyone want more coffee?" She was strict, but pleasant, not stern, and she ran the farmhouse kitchen with efficiency.

Everyone responded with a simple 'no thank-you, Ma,' except the legless veteran. He expanded his answer. "No thank-you, Mother. I lost my taste for coffee in the Army," and Billy could feel it coming.

"Did either of you gentlemen have the opportunity to serve our country in the War against the traitors of the South?" He seemed to look at Billy and Charlie at the same time.

"We sure did try. Things didn't work out real good for us. We enlisted but by the time we got assigned to an outfit the war was just 'bout over. Our home, being in Delaware, they put us with the Second Regiment of D.C. Volunteers, and we worked right there in Washington. Nothing like the action you must a seen." Billy hoped that would be enough to get him and Charlie off the spot. It wasn't.

"Knew a few boys with the Second D.C. I spent a fair amount time recovering in the hospitals in Washington. I was pretty groggy then because of my wounds. Can't recall their names but I think I remember them hailing from the area you're headed to. Stroudsville, no Stroudsburg. If I could think of their names you could call on them. I know they'd treat you kindly. So, what did your duties entail while you were with the Second?" The veteran fell silent and waited for an answer.

Billy knew he was on dangerous ground here with an experienced veteran. One slip-up and he and Orme would be exposed for the criminals they were.

"Mostly we worked in the hospitals, helping out as best we could. Once in a while they put us to guarding prisoners. Sure weren't no heroes like you." Billy hoped that would do it.

49

"Sure wish I could think of that one fellow's name. He did the same thing there as you did with the Second, and I'm sure he said he was from Stroudsburg. He held some position in the Army but I can't recall what it was. Fine man he was. Well, maybe you gentlemen will run into him up there." The wounded veteran took his eyes off Brooks and smiled at his older brother who rarely spoke and never smiled and the evening drew to a close.

The father pushed himself away from the table, rose out of his chair and spoke for the first time. "You boys take on the wood-choppin' in the morning and we'll feed you breakfast before you get on your way." He was a large man with the visible results of a life of hard work, and he wasted few words. It was his nature to make statements like the one he just uttered. You work, you eat, you leave. Brooks and Orme realized it was in their best interest to do just that.

THE BACHMAN BROTHERS

The early morning sun glistened on the smooth surface of the slow flowing Delaware River and, as always, they kept the rising sun and the river on their right. They rarely needed to consult the small compass Charlie carried. By afternoon the sun would be on their left shoulders, and that was enough directional information to keep them headed north. The town of Easton was at their backs, and each step increased their distance from it and decreased their conscious memory of it. They were done with Easton, but Easton was not yet done with them.

Warden Ezra Bachman sat at his desk and young Joshua Kern, first shift jailer, could tell he was deeply engrossed in whatever it was he was working on. He rarely looked up from his desk and he was producing a huge cloud of cigar smoke. Joshua opened the two small windows in the front room of the jail. He used the spittoon to prop open the front door and even the unflappable Bones got up and went outside.

Joshua considered inquiring into the nature of the warden's undertaking, decided against it, and went into the cell area to check on the only prisoner held that morning. The man lay on the bunk, still hours away from consciousness; Joshua contemplated why anyone would want to get that drunk.

He returned to the haze of the office where Warden Bachman seemed intent on setting himself on fire while furiously pushing his pen back and forth across a piece of official Easton Jail stationary. He could contain himself no longer.

"Anything I can help you with, Warden?"

"Nope." He tossed what was left of his cigar into the fireplace and continued. "I'm leaving now and won't be back anymore today. When Luke shows up for his shift, if Luke shows up for his shift, make sure he's informed of any situations and maybe you could stay with him for an hour or so. See that he's got a handle on things. Anything comes up that you need me for, I'll be having lunch at the Lafayette with my brother." He shook the cigar ashes off the papers and stuffed them into a large brown envelope and walked across the room to the coat rack where his large-brimmed leather hat hung.

"Very well, Warden." Joshua wanted to say something like, 'tell the Chief I said hello,' but quickly discarded the idea. He didn't want to sound phony, and besides, he was fairly confident the next patrolman position to open up would be his anyway.

Ezra stood in the foyer of the Hotel Lafayette for a minute while his eyes adjusted from the glare of the mid-day summer sun. He removed his hat and retrieved a pocket handkerchief to blot the perspiration from his face and neck. He glanced at his reflection in the full-length mirror and, satisfied with his appearance, stepped toward the door that led from the foyer to the dining room. The door opened quickly and there stood Royce, the maitre'd of the hotel, his black and white attire immaculate, as always. Royce had been around the hotel since he was a boy, washing dishes and running errands. Now, 40 years later, Royce ran the house and lived in the largest apartment on the top floor. He was such a constant that people only noticed him when he wasn't present. Most folks didn't even know his last name. Some just assumed it was 'Lafayette' and no one seemed to care that Royce was a man of color.

"Good afternoon, Warden," said Royce respectfully. "The Chief is here. I'll show you to your table."

"No need Royce. I see the rascal," Ezra said jokingly.

"Very well, Sir." And Royce discreetly disappeared.

Herman Bachman, the Chief of Police, appeared at ease and completely at home in the well-appointed dining room of one of the town's finest establishments. Almost every table was occupied by well-dressed, professional men: lawyers, doctors, merchants. A group of six men from the *Easton Express* occupied the largest table nearest the bar and were the most vocal group present. A lot of business was conducted in this dining room, usually in hushed voices by important men. Ezra recognized most of the lunch crowd and acknowledged several gentlemen as he made his way across the room to the table where Royce had seated his brother.

The Chief looked up and smiled at his younger brother. "Got a message you wanted to buy me lunch."

The Warden laughed as he lowered himself into a comfortable dining room chair. "I'll be glad to buy you lunch."

A strong family resemblance was evident in their facial features, but after that, similarities weren't as strong or as well defined. The Chief was tall and thin, the Warden short and stocky. Herman was reserved, some said stuffy. Ezra was out-going, laughed easily, and those that knew him, even for a short time, felt they had always known him. They both had a strong sense of family and community and had dedicated their lives to serving others and the city of Easton. Both had been too old for duty during the Civil War, and each had sons too young to participate, a situation they considered a blessing, then and now.

They each asked about the other's family and made some light-hearted small talk, all the while sipping a cup of the hotel's renowned turtle soup.

A tall colored man appeared beside their table. He was clad in the same black and white attire as Royce and conducted himself in the same professional manner.

"What would you gentlemen like for lunch?" He smiled and clasped his hands behind his back. Even his posture spoke of discipline.

Without hesitation Warden Bachman said, "I'll have a steak, rare, and some of those little red potatoes like I had last week."

The waiter turned his eyes to the chief, maintained the same respectful smile, and asked, "What would you like, Chief Bachman?"

"They tell me the shad just started running; did Royce put them on the menu yet?"

"He did indeed, Sir."

"Then that's what I'll have, and a small glass of Everhardt's Mead," concluded the Chief.

"Not good for a man to drink alone," declared the Warden, "I'll have a bottle of ale, and make sure it's cold."

"It will be cold, Sir." And the tall colored man walked away from the Bachman brothers.
"People think we're a lot alike, and in most ways we are, but not when it comes to the table. Never could get a taste for fish, and sure as hell not them boney old shad," the Warden said.

"A good kitchen man can take all those bones out. Our father caught and ate plenty of shad," replied the Chief.

"I do recall. I recall he also drank his share of that Mead. Always said it came from a secret recipe, made with raisins and honey and cloves. Wasn't written down and only a few people knew it. They let it ferment till you could light it."

The Warden laughed out loud.

They were served their meals and ate slowly, each enjoying the food, drink and companionship of the other.

Unaware of why his brother had invited him to lunch, the Chief's curiosity prompted him to open the conversation. "So, is there some urgent matter of police business you need to discuss with me, Ezra?"

Ezra swallowed a mouthful of steak and replied, "police matter, yes; urgent, no." He lifted his beer to his lips before continuing. "Remember them two thieves, Brooks and Orme, tried to rob Bishop's Clock Shop?"

"I do. Didn't you just turn them loose here two or three weeks ago?" The Chief raised his napkin to his face.

"I did. They headed north, up the old river road, according to Joshua. Says he watched them till they got out of sight." A hint of concern crept into the Warden's voice. "Didn't like them two. Got a feeling they're capable of worse than stealing."

The Chief stared into his brother's eyes and spoke thoughtfully, "I heard the same thing from Judge Thompson. I can't arrest them till they break the law. I guess the good thing is, they'll be breaking the law somewhere else."

"Well, that's what this meeting is about," the warden responded. "I wrote a letter warning the sheriff up there in that little town, Stroudsburg, about these two and I give him a little bit of a description. Said they ought to be showing up in early June and he should keep his eye on them. Problem is, I don't know his name or address, and I'd be obliged if you'd take a look at the letter."

"That's a hell of a gesture, little brother." There was pride in the Chief's voice. "I don't know him personally but his name is Charles Henry. Never heard anything bad about him. I think this is an election year up there in Monroe County. I suggest you address the letter to 'The Sheriff of Monroe County, Stroudsburg.' That'll get it to the station and whoever the sheriff is."

Ezra passed the letter across the table to his brother, who began reading it while the Warden drained the last remnants of ale from the dark brown bottle. He wanted his brother to read it and point out mistakes. He'd have no bad feelings about suggestions or corrections. Ever since boyhood it was acknowledged that Herman was the more erudite of the brothers. But when it came to building or repairing things around the family homestead, Ezra was the leader.

"This is real good Ezra. It'll be greatly appreciated up there." The Chief re-folded the letter and tucked it back in the envelope. "I'm going by the post office; I'll take it with me and drop it off."

"Don't forget the stamp," the Warden advised his older brother who smiled but didn't bother to respond.

Royce motioned to them as they rose from their table and both understood the gesture. Today's lunch was compliments of Royce. It didn't always work that way but Royce was a good businessman and understood the ebb and flow of the town.

They shook hands, agreed to have lunch again soon, and went their separate ways.

CATCHING A RIDE

The fragrances of early June hung in the air and the heat from the noon day sun shimmered off the dusty road. A small stream passed under an old wooden bridge and cascaded its way toward the Delaware River. They had been walking all morning and Charles Orme eyed the tumbling water with delight.

"I'm gonna have me a soak," and he made his way down the bank to the edge of the stream. His cupped hand delivered cold, refreshing water to his mouth and after quenching his thirst, he submersed his head in a pool of clear water.

William Brooks, showing no interest, stayed on the road and after several minutes called out, "Alright, let's get going."

Charlie rejoined his companion on the bridge and with a big grin on his face said, "That felt good. Used to always be jumping in the creek when I was a kid."

"Stop babbling. Look down the road," Billy said, squinting into the distance. "Wagon coming our way. Let's see if we can catch a ride."

The driver reined in the two-horse team and brought the wagon to a stop just in front of the bridge. He eyed Brooks and Orme with suspicion but did not speak. Seated next to him a large, burly man, shotgun at the ready, gruffly said, "Afternoon, boys."

"Sure would be grateful for a ride, Sir. We been walking for almost a week now." Billy maintained eye contact, knowing that looking away would create distrust.

"This here's a United States Mail Wagon. Not really allowed to take passengers." The appearance of the man riding shotgun belied a softness in his heart but not in his head. He probed, "Where you boys headed?"

"We heard tell of a little town just north of here. Stroudsburg, I think it's called. Folks say we might find work there." Billy sensed a relaxing in the men on the seat of the mail wagon.

"We got a schedule to keep, Isaac," said the man holding the reins, but it was clear to everyone that Isaac was in charge.

With his gaze still fixed on Brooks and Orme the armed man bluntly asked, "You boys fight against them rebels?"

It was a common question in the north in these post-war years. Fathers, still grieving their sons, wanted to know how and why these two healthy looking young men had escaped the carnage unscathed.

Billy resorted to one of the planned falsehoods he and Charlie had conjured up and rehearsed.

"We surely did, Sir. We was both at Cold Harbor in '64. Can't recall much about it though 'cause I got wounded in the head on the first day." Billy pointed to a small scar on the right side of his forehead, the result of a bar fight in Philadelphia last summer.

"What about him? Anything wrong with his head?" He shifted the shotgun, first pointing at Orme, then at the sky.

"Yeah, but it don't come from no fightin'," Billy smiled, Charlie looked puzzled.

"We got a schedule to keep," the driver repeated, irritation growing in his voice.

Isaac had made up his mind. "You boys can ride in the back, and don't touch nothin' in the wagon."

The driver slapped the reins against horse flesh and Billy sang out a thank-you as he and Charlie jumped aboard. Neatly arranged in the bed of the wagon were half a dozen large, well- worn leather sacks, all inscribed with the words "United States Mail." Billy and Charlie pressed their backs against the soft leather bags, stretched out their legs and felt lucky for the ride. Charlie even managed to doze-off, his shoulders nestled comfortably against the mail pouch that contained a letter to the Sheriff of Monroe County, Stroudsburg, Pennsylvania.

AT DESTINY'S DOORSTEP

Sitting peacefully on the edge of the Pocono Plateau, in the shadow of Mt. Minsi, its steep, majestic inclines covered with mountain laurel, sat the tiny, flourishing village of Delaware Water Gap. Just beneath its surface of tranquility, a burgeoning tourist industry is bubbling up. The Kittatinny House, owned and operated by Edward and John Brodhead, could already accommodate 250 guests. In July, 1855, the first telegraph message into the Gap was received at the Kittatinny from the city of Easton, further enhancing its reputation as the leading hotel in the area.

On the main road, in the center of the village, another Brodhead built and was operating a reputable establishment. Thomas, and his wife Hannah, named their hotel the Brainerd House, in honor of David Brainerd, a Moravian missionary who, in the 1740s had spread the gospel to the Native Americans living in the Minisink, a large and bountiful area of land, just north of the Water Gap.

Complimenting the hotel trade are the businesses inherent to all small but self-sufficient communities. The 390 citizens of the village have no want of gainful employment. Lumbering, a saw mill, slate cutting, brick making, farming and several large livery stables provide income for the families of the town. There's a church and a school, both constructed of the brick manufactured in the village's brick factory, and roofed with slate quarried locally and cut to size in the Gap. Additional hotels and tourist accommodations seem to spring from seeds.

Into this bucolic setting, in June, 1868, in the back of a mail wagon, Brooks and Orme arrived, at the doorstep of their destiny.

Without turning his head Isaac called out, "we're dropping off a mail bag and letting the horses drink, then we're moving on to Stroudsburg, 'bout another

5 miles. We got a schedule to keep, in case you ain't heard."

"Where we at?" inquired Billy.

Without turning to face them, Isaac answered, "Delaware Water Gap."

"Think we just gonna get out right here." Billy and Charlie jumped from the wagon and called out, "Much obliged."

This time Isaac did turn his head, and his tone was serious. "Good luck to you."

MY NAME'S RUTH

The human heart is imbued with many traits; among them are decency and virtue, neither of which were in any great supply with William Brooks and Charles Orme. They were, however, good at adapting to any situation they found themselves in, and could, when it served their purposes, be agreeable, if not almost pleasant. They stood for a few minutes, gathering their thoughts and getting their bearings. Dust rose from the street as several carriages and buggies rolled by, also on their way to the post office.

"Let's just walk on down this street and see what we come to," Billy said, and as usual, Charlie followed. They ambled past the church, perched on a rise well above street level and on the opposite side, a small brick school house sat, trimmed by mountain laurel and wild violets.

Near the bottom of the hill the street crossed the Cherry Creek and in the middle of the bridge a colored woman and two small boys were trying, without success, to get a mule to complete the crossing. Billy and Charlie approached her and Billy, smiling, addressed her, "Morning, M'am."

"Boys," she responded with exasperation in her voice.

"My friend can get him goin' for you. Charlie, get that ol' mule movin'."

Charlie took hold of the heavy rope on the mule's face that passed for a bridle and began walking. Much to everyone's surprise, including the mule, but not Charlie, the animal followed him across the bridge and back onto the main street.

"My name's Billy. I'm pleased to make your acquaintance. That there's Charlie."

"My name's Ruth, Ruth Huff and these boys are my sons. That's Amos, he's the oldest, and that little one is his brother, Ogden. And we sure are happy you boys come along when you did."

A small, rutted lane, flanked by towering evergreens, ran at a right angle to the main thoroughfare and Charlie, pointing toward it, asked, "Down this way?"

"Yes, please," the woman responded with gratitude.

The lane ran straight for about 100 feet, then gently curved right, back toward the village and along the Cherry Creek, for another 100 feet and ended in the front yard of a small but well-maintained house. In close proximity was the largest garden Brooks and Orme had ever seen, an outhouse, a shed for the mule, a coop for chickens, a smokehouse and a shanty that served whatever purpose was most needed. Every building had a slate roof.

"I surely do appreciate your help with that old mule. I'm gonna fetch you boys somethin' to eat." Turning her attention to her young sons, who appeared to be about 8 or 9 years old, she instructed them, "Amos, Ogden, you say thank-you to these men for helping us, then make sure that mule got water."

"Thank you," they said in unison, then turned and headed for the stream. They rolled an old wooden bucket in front of them, and stopped often to pick-up a stone, dropping it in the same pocket that carried their sling-shots. All creatures, furred or feathered, gave the Huff brothers a wide berth. They were the definition of mischievous.

Mrs. Huff was generous, providing a lunch of bread and smoked venison. A bottle of clear liquid with a distinctive fruity fragrance that she called 'Apple Jack' was quickly downed by Billy and Charlie.

After eating, Amos and Ogden again disappeared into a stand of birch trees near the stream. The three adults left the kitchen and walked outside. Billy and Charlie followed Ruth to the shade of two apple trees, heavy with blossoms and the promise of a bountiful autumn harvest. Billy had begun formulating a plan as soon as he saw the woman on the bridge and he decided now was the time to implement it. He started gathering information.

"This is a fine-looking property you got here, Mrs. Huff. Mr. Huff must be right proud of this homestead."

"There is no Mr. Huff. He was killed in battle in '64. A place called Olustee. That's down in Florida. Name was Amos. He had a brother, Ogden, fell there on the same day." Her voice was full of remembrance, sorrowful but not expecting pity.

"Sure am sorry to hear that, M'am." Billy was at his sympathetic best.

"Them boys looked so handsome in their uniforms. They was so proud to serve. They was in Company K, 8th Pennsylvania. All of them was colored men. United States Colored Troops. That's how they was known." Pride off-set the sorrow in her tone and she continued. "Amos be buried over in the Stroudsburg Cemetery, in a special section for colored troops. Me and the boys go on over there often as we can. We take flowers."

Billy held back from speaking. This was working out better than he had planned.

"Terrible shame about his brother, Ogden. The Army couldn't never tell us anything about what happen to his remains. Just told us he was killed. He didn't have no family, just us. I'd sure feel better knowing he got a decent Christian burial, but I guess I'll never know."

Billy quickly decided to interject. "You don't have to fret. I seen what happens when a man can't be identified. He gets a respectful burial in a nice cemetery. He gets buried in the north part if he's a yank, and in the south part if he was a reb."

"But if a man can't be identified, how they gonna know what part he belongs in?" Ruth was truly concerned for her brother-in-law's remains.

"Well, if you don't mind me telling it, they check his undergarments. Wool, he goes in the north section, cotton, he goes in with the southern boys." Billy could tell he had given Ruth a small portion of comfort and he felt good for having done it. Instinct told Billy it was time. "You know Mrs. Huff, me and Charlie just got here a little while ago. We come up from Easton. Got a ride on the mail wagon and we got nowhere to go. I was thinking, if you give us a place to sleep, we'd be happy to help out around here, just till we get ourselves settled. We wouldn't be no trouble."

"I know you boys wouldn't be no trouble, and I surely could use some help." She was hesitant but decided in favor of the arrangement. "Best I can do for quarters is that old shack."

"That ol' shack will do me and Charlie just fine." Billy felt a sense of accomplishment.

Summer settled into Delaware Water Gap and Billy and Charlie settled into the Huff homestead.

For all their coarseness they were not without an appreciation for the natural beauty of their surroundings and often walked along the mountain trails. They became familiar with the locations of small lakes, and knew where the waterfalls dropped their clear, cold water into pools formed from centuries of erosion.

At times their wanderings required strenuous effort. Rocks and boulders, left in place by the Wisconsin Glacier, made meandering difficult, if not dangerous in places. The reward of scaling these natural obstacles was a view of the river as it cut its way between Mt. Tammany and Mt. Minsi.

Not following any trail, and making use of the small compass that Charlie always carried, they made their way over the mountain at its highest point, and came out on the Cherry Creek, about two miles south of the village. They followed the creek and finally arrived back in town where Charlie, sweating profusely, collapsed in the shade of a giant sycamore tree.

Breathing heavily, Charlie spit out the words. "That's enough. Why did we have to do all that damn walking in one damn day, and in the hottest part of the day, at that?" There was irritation in his voice.

"Cause," Billy responded calmly and with a knowing confidence, "it's always good to know your surroundings." He had no idea how prophetic those words were.

RISK, REWARD, AND OPPORTUNITY

As with all occupations, being a thief requires certain skills, and one of them is being able to spot opportunity. Another is an ability to correctly measure the risk versus reward factor. Billy was pretty good at both and had determined that this little town, referred to as "The Gap" did not hold enough opportunity and carried too much risk. He would prove himself correct soon.

June slipped into July and Charlie and Billy became comfortable in a routine of working sporadically, collecting enough pay for a bottle of whiskey and helping out around the Huff place in exchange for food and lodging. Charlie contributed to the family's food supply by engaging in a favorite activity of the two small boys, Amos and Ogden. Early in the morning the boys would barge into the shack, wake Charlie from his alcohol-induced slumber and together they would proceed along a well-worn path to a spot along the Cherry Creek. They each selected a good, sturdy stick and Charlie expertly shaved a sharp point on one end. They removed their shoes, rolled-up their pants and began spearing frogs, sliding each one off the spear and into an old wooden bucket. This endeavor continued until the bucket was full or the frogs got smart enough to move on. All of them enjoyed the frog-leg dinners.

Billy ate frog legs though he didn't help catch frogs and he was growing restless. He needed some new incentives, some new activities. There had been much talk recently of a celebration. The Fourth of July was just a day away and Billy heard that the town of Stroudsburg was planning a parade to honor the men of Monroe County that had served in the Union Army. In addition to a parade, local newspapers and broadsides invited one and all to come out and enjoy music and dancing. Some of the hotels in town would provide food and drink and, in the evening, there was to be a display of fireworks. Billy knew opportunity when he heard it.

The sun dipped below the horizon and the soft glow of twilight silently filled the tiny village. Brooks and Orme sat motionless on straw-filled mattresses in their tiny, dirt-floor shack. The moon cast eerie shadows that played in the gathering darkness; an air of excitement permeated the county as folk, young and old, looked forward to tomorrow's celebration.

Charlie removed his boots and trousers, stretched out on the mattress and, half seriously stated, "That catching frogs be hard work. Takes a lot out of a man."

Billy, unamused, began a lecture. "Listen to me, fat ass. We got to have our wits about us tomorrow. We don't want to be drawing no attention to us. I don't want any lawmen asking us any questions about anything. There's gonna be soldiers there so no bragging about battles we wasn't in. Just stick to our story. We was wounded at Cold Harbor and then went to the hospital in Washington. 'Fore we got better, the war ended. You got it? And stay away from the women."

"I hear tell there's gonna be beer and whiskey for the takin'." Charlie sounded like a child on Christmas Eve.

"And another thing," Billy continued, "we gotta take a good look around and see if there ain't some places we can hit next time we go to this

Stroudsburg place. There's gotta be more stores and stuff there than here in this little shit-hole village."

"I like this little shit-hole village," Charlie countered.

"Get some shut-eye, fat ass." And they dozed off, each with their own anticipation of the next day's celebration.

4TH OF JULY, 1868 - STROUDSBURG

The good citizens of Monroe County, realizing they had been neglectful of their Civil War veterans, pulled out all the stops for this Fourth of July. The day was comfortably warm, with a gentle summer breeze cooling the body temperatures of even the most ardent celebrators. As promised, a parade with marching bands blared out the standard patriotic martial tunes of the day, evoking civic as well as national pride. Recently purchased from the city of Easton, a hand-pump fire engine was pulled by a team of handsome, well-groomed geldings. Proudly leading the 22 men of the Phoenix Fire Department and Hose Co. #2, was Captain M. B. Posten. Young boys tramped alongside the wagon, mesmerized by the workings of the pump. Women and girls were dressed in their best finery and many of the men donned their uniforms, chests still adorned with medals and badges from the various campaigns they had fought in.

The Indian Queen and the Stroudsburg House, the town's best eating and drinking establishments, put their kitchen staffs to work, laying out food and drink for all. The town's merchants, in hopes of future sales, took the opportunity to showcase their wares and services. Churches opened their doors as well, also wanting to capitalize on the chance to sell salvation and eternal life.

The courthouse was decorated, as were most buildings, with red, white and blue bunting. The stars and stripes flew on every street corner and from every imaginable crevice of every building, bridge and lamp post.

A band played on the lawn at the courthouse square, where young and old listened and danced.

Many people, including Ruth Huff and her boys, walked from the center of town to the cemetery to pay their respects to those men who had sacrificed their lives to preserve the union and bring an end to slavery. Some stayed longer than others, but after a period of reflection and introspection, almost all returned to the revelry in the borough.

Just a five minute walk from the cemetery, down Dreher Avenue and across the wide, dusty western end of Main Street, stood the fairgrounds. They held a special attraction for men and boys, and Amos and Ogden were no exception. Their mother was not in favor of visiting the grounds, but the boys pestered her until she gave in. There, horses raced and men placed bets, but the boys were too young to have any interest. They just liked to see the horses running at full gallop. The real fascination for the young brothers was in the field just beyond the track. There, a group of men and boys, led by a young attorney named David Lee, had formed teams and were playing baseball. Amos and Ogden knew that a real bat and real ball couldn't be had, but the resourcefulness of youth always finds a way around obstacles and limitations. They would play baseball anyway, with sticks and stones.

At the other end of Main Street, about a mile from the fairgrounds, several men from the fire department stood atop a rise, locally known as 'sleepers' knob', and began preparing an assortment of small explosives for fireworks, the night's climax of this Fourth of July celebration. The booms and sparks from the exploding, miniature rockets could be seen and heard for miles. It had been a wonderful day and the citizens of Monroe County were proud of their veterans for their gallant service, and proud of themselves for recognizing it.

The following morning, at all houses of worship, male attendance sharply declined. Along Main Street, church bells pealed, further paining the hung-over men who lived close by. The Methodists suffered the fewest losses, followed by the

Presbyterians, while the Lutherans counted the greatest number missing in action.

The town seemed to function in slow-motion through Sunday afternoon as hotels, businesses, and volunteer clean-up crews returned the borough to a state of cleanliness and order.

MONDAY MORNING MEETING

Charles Henry was a good man, and a good sheriff. Tall and muscular, with a full beard and mustache, he was plain spoken and self-disciplined. He expected a high degree of excellence in the performance of duties from all policemen and deputies under his command. He was strict and fair, but when expectations weren't met, dismissal was pretty much guaranteed. But if there was no malfeasance, he always helped find new employment.

He maintained a small office in the town jail on Seventh Street, just a few doors north of Main Street and a stone's throw south of the courthouse. He could have claimed a larger, more comfortable office in the courthouse, but he felt a conflict of interest might be construed by close proximity to the judges and the attorneys. Besides, he considered them to be a pain in the ass.

The early morning sun was on his back as he strode briskly along Main Street from his home near the Brodhead Creek. He knew today would be sticky and hot, and he also knew, from experience, that heat could bring out the worst in folks. He made a mental note to mention that in the meeting he held every Monday morning with police officers, deputies, the warden, his one clerk and, of course, the janitor of the jail, the aging Mr. Troch.

"Alright boys, gather 'round. Listen up. I gotta couple things to go over with all of ya," and he seated himself at his desk while the others jockeyed for position in the small office of the town jail.

"First I want to say you boys did a good job on Saturday. That was a hell of a big crowd and you did good to maintain the peace. I was surprised we didn't have to lock nobody up." Sheriff Henry gave a collective nod of appreciation to the men gathered in the small room.

"We didn't have to lock nobody up 'cause we sent 'em home with their wives. Figured that was punishment enough," and everyone laughed at the young deputy's remark.

Sheriff Henry let them have their laugh. "Alright, back to business. I know you all read the letter I passed around from Warden Bachman, down there in Easton. Anybody see the two men he described, or have anything to report about them?"

Senior Deputy and incoming Sheriff Peter Merwine, spoke up. "Me and the boys been talking, and if it's alright with you Sheriff, I'll report for the group."

"Sure." Sheriff Henry practiced brevity and encouraged others to do so.

"Well, at one time or another, we all seen both of them. All through the day and all through the town. Pretty rough-looking pair of young men, but, I gotta tell ya, far as any of us could tell, they wasn't being any trouble." Peter Merwine continued, "However, we all think, being convicted thieves, that they was, more than likely, looking for places to rob sometime in the future. We'll just have to keep an eye on them."

"Right, sounds good. Thanks for the report Pete." Sheriff Henry was proud of his people and had faith in all of them. "Now one more thing. I understand the boys from the fire company give us a good ass-kicking at horse-shoes on Saturday. That about right?"

Groans and muted laughter, but there was no denying it. They had been beaten badly by the boys from the firehouse. In an attempt to justify their poor performance, Peter Merwine spoke up. "Them old boys got more time to practice," and a general muttering of agreement sounded among the men gathered in front of Sheriff Henry's desk.

"Maybe you boys will do better next year," Sheriff Henry said encouragingly. "Let's get out on the street, and keep a sharp look-out. People can get mighty cantankerous in this heat. If you see trouble, if you need help, blow your whistle." He pushed himself out of his old ladder-back chair, indicating the meeting was over and the men under his command turned and left the jail. And, they had been right. Brooks and Orme were casing the merchants of Stroudsburg and planning future robberies. Billy had managed to lift a handful of cartridges from a hardware store for his Colt pistol and no one noticed. Billy decided then and there that he'd be back again.

CHAPTER III: MURDER AND MAYHEM

TIME TO MOVE ON

Summers have a way of passing quickly in the pleasant fields and forests of the Pocono Plateau, and this summer of 1868 was no exception. Excessive heat spells came and went with thunderstorms drenching the area from time to time. Industry continued to expand and farms delivered the bounty of fruits and vegetables to the hotels for the dining enjoyment of summer visitors. From the nearby streams came the delicacy of fresh caught mountain brook trout. Grudgingly, long peaceful days of summer relinquished some of their time to earlier sunsets and cooler nights. Work now centered around the coming winter. Woodpiles, smokehouses and root cellars grew larger. "Putting-up" an inventory of foodstuffs became the daily chore.

Billy and Charlie stayed on at the Widow Huff's, but their contributions became less and less frequent. Ruth Huff gave some consideration to asking them to move on, but her boys had grown fond of Charlie and she knew neither Amos nor Ogden would understand. Besides, times were when she was thankful for what little help Brooks and Orme provided.

The citizens of the Gap maintained their schedules throughout the seasons, instinctively understanding that there is order in routine. Roosters always crowed the dawn; church bells called the faithful. Tiny tree toads, called peepers, trilled the twilight. The rhythm and rhyme of life always promised a tomorrow. August hurried its way into September and the pace of life slowed the village down.

By mid- September, Billy was ready to travel and even Charlie had grown bored and ready to move on, although he had no idea of what to move on to. He and Billy had made several successful forays into Stroudsburg, stealing an item here and there and selling it for cash or trading it for whiskey. Charlie fashioned a bat from a hickory branch and Widow Huff stuffed straw and horsehair in a piece of leather, and sewed it into a ball so Amos and Ogden could play baseball. The boys would disappear to a remote field for hours at a time.

Billy and Charlie sat in the shack, the cool night air surrounding them. The last notes of the much-loved song, 'Lorena', drifted down Main Street from the lawn of the Kittatinny, well played by the town's band.

"I always did like that tune," Charlie reminisced. "Reminds me of our days in Washington City. We did good there in them hospitals, takin' whatever we wanted from them boys what was all shot up. 'Member how we used to put on the uniforms from the dead ones, then walk around like we was soldiers?"

"Sure, I remember. Those were the good ol' days." Billy's tone was flat, uninterested. His mind was busy planning for the future, not recalling the past.

"Ya know, Billy, last time we was in Stroudsburg, I seen something in a newspaper 'bout two railroads comin' together. Says you can ride all the way out to a place called California. Suppose to be nice all the time there. And there's an ocean. I ain't never seen no ocean. I'd sure like to see an ocean." Charlie got up from his mattress, walked to the door of the shack and watched the black bats tumble and turn in the twilight.

"We're not going to California. We're going to New Jersey. There's an ocean there you can look at." Billy always had a plan.

"Really?" Geography wasn't Charlie's long-suit.

"Listen to me." Billy needed to bring Charlie back to the present. "Tomorrow morning, we go back to Stroudsburg. We stroll into that little hardware store and we stroll out with some tools and a handful of bullets for my Colt. We come on back here and lay low for the rest of the day. Then, next morning we go on up the street to that place called the Brainerd House. That guy should buy the tools.

He's always outside sawing and hammering. If that don't work, we go on up the road to that big place everybody calls the 'Kit,' and see if we can make the sale there. By noon we should have a pocketful of money."

"Sounds good, Billy." Charlie always agreed.

Billy continued. "Then we walk, nice and easy, along the railroad tracks, hop the train when we can, and in a couple hours you'll be looking at an ocean. What do you think about that, fat ass?"

As far as William Brooks could tell, everything seemed to be going according to plan. They had arrived in Stroudsburg around mid-morning and with just enough foot traffic in the stores and on the sidewalks to make stealing and fading away unnoticed an easy task. By noon they had enough merchandise in their pants and inside the lining of their heavy shirts that they decided to head home early. They hitched a ride with a boy driving a wagon down to Slateford Farms, just south of the Gap. They jumped from the wagon as it rolled across the bridge over the Cherry Creek, then hurried down the path to their little shack on the Huff Homestead. Billy was proud of himself. He felt confident. He had pulled off the morning robberies without any difficulties even though he was aware, as he had been, that he and Charlie were being watched. He had no respect for law and order and he had even less for the men in uniform who were sworn to uphold it. He inwardly laughed at their silly hats, their long jackets and shiny badges. He loathed their straight-laced attitudes and their high 'n mighty demeanors. Although they might have suspected him, they never caught him in the act or even came close. An air of self-assuredness flowed from William Brooks. But, as with most crimes and criminals, there's always a weak spot. One small, over-looked element that eventually brings the house down. Once inside their tiny shack, they grabbed a bottle of whisky and celebrated the morning's success, blissfully unaware they had been observed and would soon be reported to Sheriff Henry by the person they least concerned themselves with and, in fact, hadn't even noticed.

WALLACE'S HARDWARE STORE – SEPTEMBER 25, 1868

Mr. Wallace was an old man, but surprisingly spry for his age and he ran his local hardware store with great success, attending to every detail of his business. He knew his customers by name, anticipated their wants and needs, and treated his employees fairly. Located at the lower, eastern end of Main Street, at an intersection locally referred to as 'five points,' Mr. Wallace watched the town of Stroudsburg grow and was proud to be playing a part in its prosperity. Among his many insights, Mr. Wallace understood the importance of mentoring the young in the town. Every spring he would hire boys to work in the hardware store, teaching them the rudiments of business, a knowledge of tools, and the fundamentals of good citizenship. His favorite saying he liked to tell all young men who worked for him was: "Not enough to work hard, you gotta work smart, too." More than a few successful men in town got their start at Wallace's Hardware Store.

Young Charles Staples, just turned fifteen, had begun working at the store that spring, the day school let out. He was a bright boy, always polite, pleasant and well-mannered. He was outgoing and cheerful and by late summer had gained a thorough knowledge of tools, had a reputation of integrity and was trusted by all who came in contact with him. Mr. Wallace had noticed, as they were closing up the shop on the evening of the September 24, that Charles seemed sullen, his typical cheerfulness replaced by the look of a boy whose dog just died. Mr. Wallace decided to let it go and see what tomorrow would bring.

The next morning young Charles Staples entered the store looking worse than he had when he left the night before. He dragged himself through the morning, nervous and jumpy and, finally, Mr. Wallace intervened. Mr. Wallace would have done the same for any of his boys, but Charles was a little special. Since Charles had come to the store in the spring, seeking employment, his eagerness put him a step ahead of the others right off. Also, Mr. Wallace knew the family. The father was a well-respected minister and his oldest brother, John Summerfield, had served in the Union Army as

President Lincoln's representative recruit. Young Charles came from good stock.

He took Charles around the counter and behind the scales used to weigh out nails and there he addressed him. "Alright son, I can see you're carrying a heavy load. What's eatin' at ya?"

There was no holding back. Charles needed to tell his story. "I done wrong, Mr. Wallace. I was scared, real scared and I done wrong. I'm ashamed of myself, and I'm sorry."

"Tell me what happened. You'll feel better." Mr. Wallace had understanding in his voice, but he also wanted to get this matter cleared up.

"I seen two men, yesterday, late in the morning. They was stealing and I could see the pistol in the coat of one of 'em. I think it's them two that everybody's been talking about. I was afraid. I was afraid he'd start shootin' if I said anything. I didn't say nothin', so they got away. I'm sorry." Young Charles Staples looked at the floor, his face red and hot with shame.

"Alright now son. You did the right thing. We can't have people turning the store into a shooting gallery. You buck-up now; everything's gonna work out."

Mr. Wallace sent one of the older clerks to fetch Sheriff Henry, and as luck would have it the sheriff was on his way to the jail, just then passing by the hardware store. He joined Mr. Wallace and Charles behind the scales and Charles repeated his story to the sheriff.

"Good boy," Sheriff Henry blurted out, almost laughing. "I got a bunch of professional lawmen out lookin' for those two sons-a-bitches, and a young boy finally sees 'em in the act." He was talking to Mr. Wallace and young Staples at the same time. "We'll go round 'em up and once they're in the jail I want the boy to come over and identify 'em." He now spoke directly to Charles. "Will you be able to do that son?"

"Yes Sir." Charles felt the question cast a shadow on his bravery and he determined to rectify that. Once the men were apprehended, he would go to the jail and point them out, decidedly and without hesitation.

SHOULD BE ROUTINE

Sheriff Henry called together a few of his most trusted deputies, including Peter Merwine, and explained the situation at the hardware store and his talk with young Staples. He didn't elaborate; he didn't need to. They had learned that Brooks and Orme were holed-up on the Huff farm several weeks ago and the goal, for right now, was to go over to the Gap and apprehend two petty thieves, then return Mr. Wallace's stolen merchandise. As is the case in small towns like Stroudsburg, word has a way of spreading quickly. It came as no surprise to the small posse when they were joined by a reporter from the *Jeffersonian-Republican*, the town's weekly newspaper. "Mind if I ride along, Sheriff?" called out Elliot Kessler, a young man in his mid-twenties, eager for a good story. Sheriff Henry didn't bother responding. He considered newspaper people to be a bigger pain in the ass than lawyers. Elliot was a capable reporter with a nose for news and a knack for being in the right place at the right time. He constantly probed and questioned, and examined every minor detail about everything. He was naturally annoying.

With their horses at a walk, the posse crossed the McMichaels Creek at 'five points' and headed for the Gap. No one was particularly worried. Although they knew one of the boys was armed, they had him out-gunned five to one. This should be a routine apprehension and arrest.

Brooks and Orme were also on the move. As planned, they strolled into the Brainerd House, an establishment half-way up the Main Street hill, and stood at the bar. Two young girls in aprons greeted them pleasantly and called for the bartender who came out of the kitchen, positioned himself behind the bar and asked what he could do for them. He masked his suspicion, just in case these two turned out to be legitimate, but he was sure they were trouble.

"Couple of whiskeys." Billy put on his sociable face.

"There's no liquor in this establishment. Down by the river there's a bar where the raft men drink, they got liquor there." Just a hint of nervousness had crept into the bartender's voice, but he was determined not to show any fear.

Billy laid a dollar bill on the bar. "We hear different."

Liquor was available, but it was held in reserve for the best customers and those who knew that well-tipped bartenders were always willing to pour. He smiled knowingly and reached for the dollar, but Billy was faster and brought his right hand down, covering the bill. "When I see the whiskey." The bartender disappeared to the storage area along with the two aproned girls.

That was all the experienced team of Brooks and Orme needed. They went right for the cash drawer, breaking it open and stuffing the money inside a bag that also held the stolen tools. Unhurriedly they walked across the dining room, out the front door and down the steps. Charlie carried the heavy sack as they strolled, side by side, just like Billy said, along the main road that led out of the village of Delaware Water Gap.

Not a full thirty seconds had elapsed from the time the bartender left to retrieve the bottle of whisky until his return, and in less than one second he realized what had just happened.

"God damn those two." His anger spilled over; he barked at the two girls to run and fetch Thomas Brodhead, the proprietor. He also knew his days of working at the Brainerd were numbered.

Thomas rushed from a nearby field where he'd been pulling weeds, loosening soil in each row of his neatly planted corn and pumpkins. Drenched in sweat and his boots covered with dust, he entered the bar area and looked directly at his bartender.

"Tell me what happened, quickly." He wasn't gruff but he was upset, and he knew time was of the essence.

After a recap Thomas asked for a description of the robbers. The bartender and the two serving girls gave the same information.

"Are they armed?" Thomas inquired.

"Didn't see a weapon, Sir." The girls didn't answer, only the bartender.

Thomas flew out of the Inn and hurried up Main Street just as his brother, Theodore was leaving the post office. Thomas ran to meet him, catching his breath before he could speak.

"Easy there brother. Here, I got your mail for you." Thomas took the packet of letters from Theodore and stuffed it in his shirt, still breathing heavily.

"Just been robbed," he finally managed to blurt out. "Cleaned out the cash drawer at the hotel. I think we might be able to catch 'em."

Theodore, shocked by the distressing news, couldn't speak for several seconds, then suggested, "Let's get on down to the train station. They might be headed out of town on the afternoon train."

They spoke with the station master, Carson Wells, who informed them that no one fitting the description of Brooks and Orme had been at the station, adding he would detain them if they showed up. They thanked him and, once outside, smiled knowingly at each other, smiled even in the face of this adversity. Mr. Wells was a diminutive man, well over eighty, with limited eye sight. His hearing had deserted him years ago, and he didn't really walk, he shuffled. He couldn't detain a snail on a good day.

The Brodhead brothers left the station and searched on and on for the two thieves. They knew their prospects of catching them and reclaiming Thomas's money were growing slimmer with each tick of the clock. Not only did Brooks and Orme have a good ten minute head start on them, but two men in their fifties were going to have a hard time catching two boys in their twenties.

Undeterred, they made their way to the Kittatinny House, where their brother, William, was proprietor. They told him about the robbery.

"They were here, and not long ago. Tried to sell me tools that I could see didn't belong to them." William became more agitated as he spoke. "I said no to buying anything from them. I'm right sure they headed down the road, towards the point of the gap. Give me a minute and I'll come with you. This country's going to hell in a peach basket."

William was angry, not just for his brother's loss but about what he saw as an outbreak of lawlessness throughout the county.

"No, William, you stay here," Thomas advised. "They might double-back. Don't leave nothing unguarded." Thomas and Theodore left the Kittatinny as their brother called out, "Good luck and be careful."

They stood in the center of the dusty road, each Brodhead brother drawing strength from the other, as they squinted into the distance. Thomas saw them first. "There. There they are. About a quarter mile out. Just walking along like innocent school boys." Thomas and Theodore set out at a brisk pace, more determined than ever now that their quarry was in sight. Slowly, but surely, the distance between the hunters and the hunted began to close.

THE POSSE

Sheriff Henry and his small group of lawmen crossed the Cherry Creek and entered the borough of Delaware Water Gap. The sound of horse hooves on old wooden bridge planks sent vibrations through the ground and into the stream; trout darted for the safety of deep holes and overhanging tree branches.

He turned in the saddle and faced the posse. "You men stay here. I'm gonna go on down this lane and talk to Mrs. Huff," and the sheriff reined his horse toward the lane, then stopped short. The keen powers of observation, inherent in the make-up of good lawmen, prompted him to call out. "You boys come down out of that tree, you hear me?" Amos and Ogden nimbly navigated the lower branches of the giant evergreen until they reached the ground and stood, wide-eyed, looking up at Sheriff Henry.

"You boys belong to Mrs. Huff?" Sheriff Henry knew who they were.

"Yes Sir. I be Amos and he be Ogden." The sheriff noted the politeness and the pride.

"You got two men living here with you?" He knew the answer to that question as well.

"Yes Sir. They come and go. Mostly go, now-a-days." Amos always spoke, he was the oldest. "They left early, don't know where they headed."

Paternal instinct or fatherly intuition, or some combination of both, Sheriff Henry had a feeling these two could get themselves in the middle of something that could result in injury or worse. He spoke to them in a serious tone. "I need you boys to stay here on this bridge. Keep a sharp eye on anyone that crosses. I'm making you both 'Special Deputies.' Your orders are to stay right here. Understood?"

"Yes, Sir!" Their excitement knew no bounds.

VIOLENT ENCOUNTER

Thomas Brodhead reached Brooks and Orme first. Hearing the heavy footfalls behind them, they turned in unison, and from behind a mask of civility, Billy said, "Afternoon."

"I believe you boys have some money that belongs to me," Thomas stated firmly. "You're both going back to town. We're gonna clear this up." He was out of breath but determined; no fear was evident in his voice as he reached out and grabbed both Billy and Charlie by the sleeves of their dirty coats.

Billy correctly reasoned that if he put his captor at ease, the opportunity to escape would eventually present itself so he said, "Very well, I'll go back to town with you."

Charlie, never the quick thinker, emphatically stated he wasn't going. When Thomas turned his gaze toward Charlie, Billy quickly picked up the bag containing the stolen money and tools and attempted to throw it over a nearby stone wall. It was a feeble attempt at hiding evidence. The bag hit the wall and paper dollars floated in the gentle, late summer breeze, coming to rest in the dusty roadway.

Having reached the scene, Theodore dryly observed, "this must be your money, Thomas."

Emboldened by the presence of his brother, Thomas released his grip on Brooks and Orme and bent down to gather his cash. He heard his brother Theodore say, "You better not shoot," unaware that these would be his last words. Thomas straightened up, dollars bills in each hand and saw Brooks aiming a pistol at his brother, Theodore. Thomas echoed his brother's words, "Don't you shoot," making himself the first target. Brooks turned from Theodore and fired at Thomas hitting him in the left side just above the waist. The bullet from the Colt tore through his jacket, then his shirt, then slowed as it passed through the packet of letters his brother had handed him just a short time ago. The bullet tumbled as it exited the letters and opened a gaping hole in Thomas' side. Blood poured. Thomas fell to his knees and saw Brooks turn the gun back at Theodore. Billy's second shot hit Theodore mid-chest and split his heart in half. He was dead before he hit the ground.

"Damn you both," Thomas cried out, as he slowly rose, his left hand covering the hole in his side and rapidly filling with blood. Orme grabbed the pistol away from Brooks and fired a shot at Thomas, grazing the right side of his forehead, sending him back to his hands and knees. Blood ran down his face and into his eyes. He stood again and lurched forward. Off-balance from the gunshot wounds, weak and unable to see, he stumbled into Orme, who then fired off the three remaining rounds, missing Thomas each time. He clung to Orme with all the strength he had left, sending Orme into a panic and prompting him to yell to Billy, "Get a rock and beat his brains out!" Billy brought the rock down on the head and face of Thomas Brodhead until blood flowed from his ears and nose. Both eyes swelled and closed. Everything above his shoulders had been turned into a mass of bloody pulp. Thomas surrendered to the pain and loss of blood, sank into the oblivion of unconsciousness, and waited to join his brother, Theodore, in death.

UNCLE THEODORE'S BEEN KILLED

The retort of the gunfire ricocheted off Mt. Minsi, bounced along the river, tumbled down Main Street, and dissipated into the warm afternoon air. Nervous and skittish, the horses reared, startled by the sound. Deputies reined in their mounts and one yelled, "What the hell?" He was answered by another, "Maybe just boys squirrel huntin'."

Sheriff Henry knew better. He knew the sound of gunfire and he knew those shots came from a pistol, not a rifle. An eerie feeling invaded his inner being; those shots were fired in anger; images of Shiloh flashed in his memory's eye.

Sound has a way of bouncing around in mountainous terrain, making it difficult to pinpoint the source of the noise.

Peter Merwine asked the first logical question. "Where do you think, Sheriff?"

"Hard to say. Best guess is due east. Up the main road, maybe a mile, maybe two." The Sheriff called out, "Single file, fire only if fired on, and you," pointing at the young reporter, "are to stay out of the way." He spurred his horse and started up the main road, followed by Merwine, the three deputies and the reporter, who was not going to be denied a good story. It seemed that this was not going to be a routine arrest after all.

The sheriff and his men passed through the village without incident and made their way along the grounds bordering the Kittatinny House. Near the end of the property, in the shade of a large sycamore tree, a man was kneeling over something lying in the grass, unidentifiable at this one hundred yard distance.

"Go check it out, Pete. Probably nothing, but go have a look." Sheriff Henry shifted his weight in the saddle and called out to the others, "Hold up."

Peter Merwine rode quickly to the sycamore tree, dismounted and walked to the kneeling man. He gasped, stared in disbelief for several seconds, then said, "Good Holy Jesus." Turning to the men on the road he excitedly waved them to come to him. The posse arrived and all stood motionless, shocked by the condition of the man cradled in the arms of Edward Brodhead. No one spoke; no one could. They waited for the sheriff to speak. The young reporter turned his head and vomited.

"Who is it, Edward? Is that Tom Brodhead?" Sheriff Henry knew Edward. Knew he was a nephew of Theodore Brodhead. Everybody knew everybody.

"Yes Sir," Edward replied while wiping blood from the face of the severely injured Thomas.

"Can he talk?" The sheriff asked.

"He did say a few words but he's hurt real bad. Said my Uncle Theodore been killed. Said there was two of 'em, and something about stealin'. Then he passed out."

The sheriff turned to the youngest of the deputies. "Get back to town. Round up men for a search party. Deputize some boys down at the firehouse if you have to. And get Doc Jackson over here, fast."

Wiping his mouth, the young reporter spoke up. "Wait Sheriff. I got friends in the telegraph room at the Kit. I'll get them to send a wire, it'll be much faster."

"Go do it, son." Like the kid or not, the sheriff knew a good idea when he heard one. "And send somebody up here with hot water and clean towels."

Edward looked up into the eyes of Sheriff Henry. "He's not gonna make it, is he?"

"That's up to God now. God and ol' Doc Jackson. We're going up the road and have a look around. We'll catch these two and they'll hang."

Sheriff Henry, Senior Deputy Peter Merwine and the three junior deputies started up the road. They came upon the body of Theodore Brodhead about a quarter mile from the 'Kit.' The young deputies, shaken by the sight of violent death, slowly dragged Theodore's body out of the road and placed it in the shade of some mountain laurel. They crossed the arms and gently laid them on the chest. One of the men took off his vest and placed it over Theodore's face. Sheriff Henry noted these respectful gestures.

They all began to inspect the area. Footprints in the dusty road and disturbances in the dirt, where a fight to the death had recently occurred, were observed.

Peter Merwine called out, "Over here," and the others joined him at the side of the road, where broken twigs, bent branches and foot prints in the soft soil of the forest floor indicated an intrusion. "They went in here. They're headed up the mountain. They'll leave a hell of a trail in this undergrowth. Might be able to follow 'em."

"You're right, Pete. Good work," stated Sheriff Henry. "You want us to follow 'em, Sheriff?", asked one of the junior deputies, anxious to make his mark in the department. "No, too steep and overgrown for the horses," replied the sheriff. "They won't head south, they're wanted down there. East puts them in the river. North puts them back in the village. They're moving west and I got a feeling they're familiar with the terrain. No matter. We'll catch 'em." Sheriff Henry stood by his horse and stared into the gorge, cut by the Delaware River over eons of time. He silently contemplated the serenity of nature and the violence of man. "Let's get back into town. We're gonna need to organize search parties. I don't want these folks turning into a lynch mob." They followed the sheriff to their horses. Passing by the 'Kit', they noted that both Edward and the badly mauled Thomas were no longer under the tree. Perhaps God and ol' Doc Jackson had managed to save the life of Thomas Brodhead.

Bad news seems to travel at a speed in direct proportion to the size of the town it occurs in. The smaller the town, the faster it spreads. That worked to the detriment of Brooks and Orme but was an advantage for the citizens of the Gap. In their shock and dismay, they had quickly turned out in force to capture those responsible for Monroe County's first murder.

APPREHENSION AND ARREST

Just a few steps past the Brainerd House, a small side street called Shepard Avenue intersected the main road that cut through the village. Here is where Antoine Dutot, the founder of this place he named Dutotsburg, envisioned the town square.
Although he'd been dead for 25 years, this spot did function as the town square, on those occasions when Delaware Water Gap needed a town square. Today was one of those occasions.

Positioned on an elevated mound overlooking the square, Elliot Kessler was hurriedly writing his report. All the citizens of the Gap, and surrounding area, had turned out, and were armed. The young reporter made note of several highly agitated men who were carrying a rope, already fashioned into the hangman's noose.

He hailed the Sheriff and Peter Merwine as they rode by. "Hope you men don't mind but I took the liberty of sending a telegram to the coroner."

They raised their arms in acknowledgement and Peter Merwine turned to Sheriff Henry, "You want me to shoot that little prick?" Sheriff Henry smiled and his eyebrows went up, but he remained silent.

There's a thin line between a crowd and a mob and Sheriff Henry knew that this crowd was quickly becoming a mob. He stood tall in the town square and spoke to them as their sheriff, of what he expected, and of what they could expect if the rule of law was infringed upon. He put a dozen men with each one of his deputies and gave them a specific area to search. He spoke emphatically about bringing the murdering team in alive. The law would see to justice, not revenge. He advised them to follow the lead of the deputy they were assigned to and finally, he wished them good luck. That was all he could do. Now he would have to await the outcome, and trust in the good sense of common citizens. The everyday, law-abiding men and women who were now angered and bereaved beyond their breaking point.

He didn't have to wait long. It had only been two hours since the search teams left the square when he heard the three sharp blasts of a deputy's whistle, signaling that Brooks and Orme had been apprehended. Again, he had difficulty determining where the sound came from. His guess was somewhere down Cherry Valley Road, and as it turned out, he was correct.

Billy and Charlie had made their way across Mt. Minsi and followed the downward curve of the mountain into Cherry Valley. They had taken this course earlier in the summer and Billy thought it might serve them well today, as an escape route. They cleared the dense undergrowth, crossed the road parallel to the Cherry Creek and took cover in another heavy stand of scrub oak, pine and the ever-present Mountain Laurel. There they sat, hope fading with the late day sun, until they were surrounded. They decided to surrender rather than fight it out. A wise decision considering that Billy was now out of bullets, and Charlie was just plain out of steam.

Handcuffed together, with deputies and gun-toting citizens all around them, they walked along Cherry Valley Road and entered the village at the little bridge, where Sheriff Henry had positioned his 'special deputies.'

"I'm getting my ass back up that tree so's I can see better." Amos declared.

"Sheriff said we suppose to stay on this bridge." Ogden countered.

"I don't give a damn, I needs to see." Amos emphatically stated.

"I'm gonna tell Ma you was cussin'. Then you'll get a beatin'." Ogden liked to threaten his older brother with tattling.

"Go 'head, cuz after I get a beatin' from Ma, you'll be gettin' one from me," and Ogden followed his older brother up the tree to their perch in the pines.

BACK TO JAIL – STROUDSBURG STYLE

Brooks and Orme were man-handled into the back of a buckboard wagon. They sat on the rough floorboards, despondent and scared, surrounded by deputies and firemen. They had arrived in Delaware Water Gap in the back of a wagon, and they were leaving the same way. Angry voices called out for revenge and a group of men rushed toward the wagon. Sheriff Henry understood the danger of mob mentality. He rode through the crowd, his mount frightened and rearing, knocking men to the ground. Finally, he was in ear-shot of the driver and he yelled to him. "Get 'em over to the jail. Arrest any son-of-a-bitch that tries to stop ya. I'm hangin' these two bastards myself. Go on. Pull out." He spurred his horse toward the lane that led to the Huff homestead and stopped under the tree that held Amos and Ogden.

Composing himself, he spoke in a fatherly tone. "You boys done a good job. I'm thinking to keep you on as 'special deputies' Never know when you'll be needed again." He reached in his vest-pocket, pulled out two pennies, and handed one to each of the Huff bothers. He spurred his horse to a trot and headed for the wagon carrying the two murderers.

It had been a terrible day for the citizens of Monroe County and the folks of Delaware Water Gap had been hit the hardest. Everyone would carry the memory of that day's events with them all their lives. Though all carried memories of the same event, they carried them in different packages. Amos and Ogden marked their package 'proud to have served', and carried it with them the rest of their days.

The Kittatinny Hotel: Near this hotel, Theodore Brodhead was murdered. It was operated by his brother, William, and burned to the ground in 1931. *Courtesy of the Monroe County Historical Association, Stroudsburg, Pa.*

The first shot fired by Brooks hit this pack of letters, saving the life of Thomas Brodhead. *Courtesy of the Antoine Dutot Museum, Delaware Water Gap, Pa.*

This is the hand-written verdict of the jury and their signatures. *Courtesy of the Monroe County Archives, Stroudsburg, Pa.*

John H. Abel

These men, William Brooks and Charles Orme, committed the first murder in Monroe County, Pa. *Image taken from the Stroudsburg Times, 26 Feb. 1903.*

The Brodhead Brothers: Sitting, from left to right: William, Thomas, Theodore. Standing, left to right: Luke, Horace, Benjamin Franklin, DeWitt, Lewis. *Courtesy of the Monroe County Historical Association, Stroudsburg, Pa.*

Governor John W. Geary: A General in the Union Army, he signed the warrants to hang Brooks and Orme.

CHAPTER IV:
IF BEFORE
MIDNIGHT

THE SHERIFF AND THE DOCTOR

The jail in Stroudsburg was a far cry from the jail Brooks and Orme had departed that spring. They were in big trouble this time and they knew it. Depressed and sullen, they sat in their cell and spoke very little. There were no windows to provide fresh air or a glimpse of sunlight or moonlight or trees or birds. There was no view of a leisurely flowing river. On the floor were two straw-filled mattresses, two blankets, one bucket. One pair of eyes peered relentlessly through the bars of the door, keeping a constant vigil. There were no wash days, no barber visits, no church ladies with baked goods and the Good Book. Two deputies stood guard outside the jail, 24 hours a day. The Easton jail now seemed like the good old days. Bitterly, the words of the young Easton jailer, Joshua Kern, burned in their ears: "Old boys up there don't take to stealin'."

In the three days since the murder, Sheriff Henry had been in and out of his office frequently, busy with post-crime reports, writing a letter to Warden Bachman in Easton, and seeing to the day-to-day business of being sheriff. He took time to congratulate his people on their fine performance in the field. Mr. Schock, editor of the local paper, received a letter commending the actions of his young reporter, Elliot Kessler, acknowledging that his idea to send a telegram from the Kittatinny had helped save the life of Thomas Brodhead. By late afternoon he felt confident in leaving the jail in the hands of his deputies, and rising from his desk, informed those present, "Alright boys, I'm going to see Doc Jackson."

"You feeling bad, Boss?" That came from the youngest and newest of the deputies, still unfamiliar with office protocol.

Sheriff Henry was addressed as "Sheriff Henry" - not "Chief," not "Boss."

He smiled and raised his eyebrows as he pulled the door shut, knowing that the more experienced would enlighten the young man.

The home and office of Doctor Reeves Jackson was at the corner of Sarah and Eighth Street, and the Sheriff covered the distance in less than five minutes. He knew the doctor well and had a great admiration for him, both as a doctor and as a citizen of Stroudsburg. On the few occasions when he was feeling ill, he went to see Doc Jackson, and always came away feeling better. With no front porch, just a step-up from the sidewalk, Sheriff Henry knocked his boots against the step, then lifted the door-knocker and tapped twice. The late afternoon sun glanced off the dusty street; it was warm for late September. He didn't wait long before the front door swung open and Doctor Jackson greeted him cordially.

"Come in Sheriff. I've been expecting you." He was a slight man, in his mid-fifties, with silver hair, always clean-shaven, always with refined manners. He was even-tempered, trusted, and respected.

"Well, if you been expecting me, then maybe you know why I'm here." Sheriff Henry smiled, hoping for good news.

"Let me start like this: Thomas will live, far as I can tell. Just saw him again, early this morning. But he won't be the same Thomas Brodhead we've known. He's got a lot of mending to do and that's going to take some time, maybe more than he's got left." The doctor walked to a large, overstuffed chair, seated himself, and signaled Sheriff Henry to take the smaller chair opposite him.

"What do you think about his mind?" The sheriff's tone was more serious now.

Doctor Jackson stared into the sheriff's eyes and took a moment before responding. "He'll be able to testify."

Satisfied with the results of his visit, Sheriff Henry rose and the Doctor followed suit.

On his way to the door the sheriff asked, "And how was your European trip? Enjoyable I trust."

"Most enjoyable. Met a writer named Samuel Clemens. Goes by the pen-name Mark Twain. Interesting fellow. Provided my wife and me with many humorous tales."

"I'll see you tomorrow at the cemetery?" asked the Sheriff.

"I'll be there. Unless somebody decides to have a baby." They smiled at each other in mutual respect, then parted company. Doc Jackson had concerns about hanging men. He had even greater concerns about hanging boys. He wanted to broach the subject with the sheriff, but he knew this wasn't the time or place, and he understood, correctly, that it wasn't up to Sheriff Henry, so he let it pass.

THE BURIAL OF THEODORE BRODHEAD

No one had ever been murdered in Monroe County before, so this service and burial of a prominent citizen was going to take some planning. Everyone wanted to do it right, and everyone recognized that the Presbyterian Church in the Gap couldn't even begin to accommodate the anticipated number of mourners. All the leaders of all the churches met and coordinated their plans so as to pay proper respect to one of the area's leading citizens. After a week of meetings and endless hours of discussion, it was decided that in order to allow everyone to pay homage to Theodore Brodhead, each area church would hold a memorial service on Sunday, October fourth, and after those individualized services, anyone wishing to do so could attend the burial in the Delaware Water Gap cemetery.

William Brodhead, brother of Theodore, and proprietor of the Kittatinny House, laid out food and beverage for the more than three hundred mourners who solemnly made their way from the cemetery, down the hill, then up to the hotel. Most ate and drank in respectful moderation. A few didn't. Many recalled the words of Theodore's mother. She enjoyed telling she had given birth to eight boys, all of whom had grown to more than six feet tall. She joked she had forty eight feet of sons. She never spoke those words again.

The weather was kind to the mourners of Monroe County on this solemn Sunday afternoon. The sun shone gently from a clear, azure sky. The first hints of autumn whispered in the cool breeze and tinge of color in the leaves. People gathered in groups inside the Kittatinny, on the veranda, and out in the lawn. Under a spreading Chestnut, three men stood together conversing in the tone of those who had seen war but rarely spoke of it. They were not close friends but they all knew each other and were certainly friendly. The death of Theodore Brodhead brought them together; they took the opportunity to renew their acquaintance.

After handshakes, and a few general comments regarding the recent tragedy, they stared at each other through several seconds of awkward silence.

At forty two years of age, Lewis Long, a farmer from Analomink and older than the other two, took it upon himself to open the dialogue.

"Nice to see you boys, again, unfortunate circumstances notwithstanding," he began.

"Nice to see you Mr. Long," William Walton responded. William didn't know Lewis very well, and just twenty nine years old, decided to address the senior gentleman as 'Mr.'

Somewhat surprised by that, Lewis quickly followed up with, "Just call me Lewis, son."

Summerfield Staples, son of a local minister and the youngest of the trio, turned and spoke directly to William Walton, "You know William, Lewis and I were in the same outfit during the war, Co. C, 176th Pennsylvania. We were down in New Bern, North Carolina when I came down with the typhoid. They put me on a train and sent me home."

Lewis Long picked-up the story. "But he recovered, went back in the Army and become Abe Lincoln's representative recruit. Ain't that something? He never got the proper recognition for that."

"I got recognized enough. Just glad the war's over," and the other two men voiced agreement with Summerfield.

"You lads planning to stay here, in Monroe County?" inquired Lewis.

"Just got a job with the Stroudsburg Post Office," William said through a proud smile, "so I'll be here in town."

"Just hired on with the Delaware, Lackawanna and Western Railroad," Summerfield said. "I'm leaving next week for Waterloo, New York. Don't know exactly what to expect, but I think railroading's good work."

"Good for both of you, and good luck to both of you." Lewis Long pulled his watch from his vest pocket. He studied it for a second, then looked up from the face of the watch and into the faces of a younger generation. He extended his hand and with heart-felt sincerity said, "Good luck boys." He walked out of the shade of the chestnut tree and past the Kittatinny. Summerfield and William Walton watched him disappear from view.

"Think I best be gettin' on myself," William said.

"Let me talk to you for a minute." A touch of anxiety was in Summerfield's voice.

"Sure. Anything wrong?" William asked.

"I think I seen them two murderers before. You gotta keep that to yourself, please." Summerfield implored.

William was incredulous. "Where, when?"

"As you know, after I recovered I enlisted again. They put me with the 2nd DC Volunteers. I was in Washington, working in the hospitals. Late '64 till the end of the war. They would come into wards and steal from the dead and the wounded. Took money and clothes."

"You saw them do that? You're sure it was them?" Walton asked, his concern deepening.

"Yes, well, pretty sure. Never got a real good look. They always came in at night and they was quick. Only happened twice as I recall." Staples removed his hat and fanned his face.

Wanting the conversation to remain private, Walton quickly surveyed the area checking the proximity of others, then asked, "What about names?"

"Never got names. Names they're using they likely took off the dead." Staples returned his hat to his head and looked down at polished boots.

Looking up, he continued. "We put together a four man detail. Had a plan to catch 'em. A good plan. They must have figured we was on to them cause one night," he snapped his fingers, "they just vanished."

Two attractive young women strolled near-by, their black, taffeta hoop skirts brushing the manicured lawn. Both boys removed their hats, smiled pleasantly and said "Good afternoon."

When the girls had passed, Staples continued, a touch of exasperation now evident in his voice. "If we had stopped 'em then, we wouldn't be standing here now."

"Hold on there, Summerfield. You bear no responsibility for any of this," William Walton said reassuringly. He stepped closer to Staples and deeper into the shade. "I was in D.C., assigned to the 4th Pennsylvania. Worked my way up to Ward Master in the Hospital Corp. Got discharged in the summer of '64. Must have just missed you. Never did hear or see anything like what you been telling me. What are you going to do?"

"Can't say for sure. Don't rightly know. I want to do right. Been thinking I might tell Sheriff Henry." Disjointed thoughts flowed from the uncertain Staples.

"You tell anybody and you'll have to testify." Walton cautioned.

"That's where I'm over a log. I won't put my hand on a Bible and say I saw something I maybe didn't see."

"I understand."

"But if I don't testify and they go free, I'll never......"

A quick outburst of laughter from Walton interrupted the concern of Staples.

"Those two aren't going free, my friend, whether you testify or not."

Staples smiled in understanding and felt relieved having shared his heavy burden.

"Still, this thing is a stone in my boot," admitted Staples.

"Think of it this way. There's no harm gonna come from not speaking up. No harm at all, and no difference will be made if you do." Having offered his best, heart-felt advice, Walton silently stared into the face of his friend.

"It does eat at me but I believe you are right, William."

With gentle authority Walton concluded, "Then it is settled. It shall remain with us and today shall be the end of it."

They shook hands and ambled back to the hotel to pay their respects to the surviving members of the Brodhead family.

Staples never shared his recollections with anyone other than William Walton but often pondered his decision to keep silent.

On a bitter cold afternoon in January 1888, the matter was laid to rest, along with the body of John Summerfield Staples.

No one ever found out that three years prior to murdering Theodore Brodhead, Staples had witnessed William Brooks and Charles Orme desecrate the dead and dying soldiers of the Army of the Potomac.

THE DEFENSE TEAM ASSEMBLES

The brilliant colors of a Pocono October bled away into the muted grey of November. December brought short, cold days; snow fell across the plateau, providing a delight for children and a distinct advantage for hunters. Fires blazed in the hearths of homes and hotels throughout the area. A feeling of security descended, like snowflakes, on the residents of Monroe County.

Brooks and Orme were also secure. They were secure in the Stroudsburg jail, under guard night and day, with little in the way of distraction. They were frequently hungry and always cold. In early December, their boredom was punctuated by visits from a three-man defense team, attorneys who would make every effort to save them from the gallows. Although not enamored with the task of representing the two most hated men in the county, attorneys Burnett, Storm and Lee, were determined to do a credible job while maintaining the respect of the community.

Snow fell from a cloud covered sky as the three lawyers made their way up Seventh Street for their 10am meeting with Sheriff Henry. They stomped snow off their boots, then entered the jail and found the sheriff standing behind his small but functional desk. After the customary greetings of men who hold each other in tempered high regard were exchanged, the defense team seated themselves in front of the desk, and Attorney Charlton Burnett opened the conversation.

Tall, well-mannered and well-dressed, he was almost regal in his personal appearance. He had been the Chief Burgess of Stroudsburg, had served as District Attorney, and at 42 years of age was the oldest and would lead the defense team. His closest friends called him 'Colonel'; a respectful reference to his rank during the Civil War.

"We will need to speak with them," he began, as Sheriff Henry listened politely. "Individually first, then together. We need to have their side of the story, and it needs to be consistent, since we understand they are to be tried together. Preferably this would be done in my office. You have my personal guarantee that they will be in the courthouse on the day of the trial."

"They aren't leaving the confines of this jail, individually or together." Sheriff Henry crossed his arms on his chest and smiled at the three attorneys.

"Very well then Sheriff. Tell us how we are to proceed." Attorney John B. Storm was going to approach this initial stand-off in a conciliatory manner. He too had distinguished himself in the early phases of the formation of Monroe County. After graduating from Dickinson Law School, he had been appointed Superintendent of Schools and for seven years steered a course of excellence in education in Monroe County. He was highly respected as a trial lawyer and was well known for his effectiveness as a public speaker. Although twelve years his junior, Charlton Burnett had invited him onto the defense team because of his ability.

"You will have access to the prisoners every day, for as long as you require," Sheriff Henry said in a cooperative voice. "They will be hand-cuffed prior to your entering their cell, which is where the meetings will take place, and a deputy will be positioned just outside the cell door." His tone now more serious, the sheriff continued, "I'm not taking any chances with these two sons-a-bitches."

At 28 years old, David S. Lee was the youngest attorney on the team. He sat quietly and respectfully, attentive to every word.

"Of course, you are correct Sheriff, and we appreciate the huge responsibility that you have here." Attorney Storm then asked if Brooks and Orme could be made available to them that morning. Sheriff Henry called for a deputy to prepare the prisoners.

TRIAL
DAY ONE
MONDAY, 28 DECEMBER, 1868

Morning arrived clear and bright and bitter cold. At dawn people lined the street from jail to courthouse. Their breath created miniature clouds of steam that mimicked the wood smoke curling from the chimneys of homes, hotels and businesses. Stroudsburg was filled with excitement, and covered with snow.

Sheriff Henry had ordered the removal of snow from walkways that led from the jail to the courthouse, a distance of about two hundred feet. He met with the Mayor and the borough council and recommended placing wooden barricades on each side of the line of travel that Brooks, Orme, and the deputies would have to navigate. Citing expense, the town fathers balked at this suggestion.

"Mob rule is a very dangerous thing, gentlemen, and there's a lot more of them than there are of us." The sheriff spoke in his most serious voice, "Be good to stop a lynching before it starts." The barricades were authorized, hurriedly built and put in place.

By 8 am the crowd had grown in size and agitation and chants of "hang 'em now, hang 'em now," erupted at several points between courthouse and jail.

The sun glanced off the hard-packed snow, sparkling and blinding, and beat its way, in piercing shafts, through the small windows of the jail. Sheriff Henry stood in the center of the room and cleared his throat before addressing the deputies who waited in nervous silence.

"We have, this morning, a difficult and dangerous task before us." His delivery was intentionally measured and solemn. Everyone understood that this was more than the usual Monday morning briefing. The Sheriff continued, "There are many people between here and the courthouse, and make no mistake, there are those who are intent on disrupting us in the performance of our duties. It is our job to deliver the two prisoners, unscathed, to the courthouse for their fair and just trial. I know you are all familiar with your assignment. Are there any questions?" The only sound in the room was the crackling of oak logs burning in the pot-bellied stove.

The sheriff looked at each man standing in the tiny, crowed jail and assessed the amount of nervous strain in their faces. He expected strain - it was natural. He was checking for fear. Fear could cause a man to over react, to misread a situation and turn a minor infraction into a deadly confrontation. Satisfied that he saw none, he turned to Senior Deputy Peter Merwine and without emotion stated simply, "You may proceed."

They had been over it a dozen times. They had even rehearsed it, using two bartenders from Stroudsburg House, to play the parts of Brooks and Orme. They were confident; they were ready. This time the stage would be real, and this first act, the most dangerous.

Mr. Troch, an old man who worked as the jail janitor, opened the door and, as practiced, Peter Merwine stepped out into the cold, crisp air, catching his breath as his lungs filled with the December morning. Behind him came a deputy with a shotgun cradled in his arms. Then two more deputies with holstered side arms. Next came

William Brooks, his arms dangling in front of him, held in place by hand cuffs that glinted in the morning sun. The heavy leg-irons at his ankles made him walk with a shuffling almost comical gait. Charles Orme, encumbered by a matching set of irons, stepped through the door next. He stopped suddenly, either from the cold or the blinding sun, but was shoved forward by the next two deputies, almost causing him to stumble. This arrangement put two deputies on the left and the right of Brooks and Orme. Last out was Sheriff Henry. A hush fell on the restless crowed which had been standing in the cold for hours. Everyone wanted a glimpse of the men who had murdered Theodore Brodhead.

It took four minutes to get to the courthouse, a distance usually covered in about forty seconds. Ugly cries called for the death of Brooks and Orme, but the disciplined group of seven lawmen and two anxious outlaws, reached their destination without incident or violence.

Peter Merwine pulled open the heavy oak door at the main entrance to the courthouse and signaled the others to enter. Several seconds of hesitation and confusion passed as the group piled up in the foyer. The worried tipstaff and the anxious bailiff, positioned at the door to the courtroom, only twenty feet down the hall, called out, "Everything alright, Sheriff?"

Peter Merwine took the question. Blinking furiously, he answered, "We're all snow-blind."

Austere, the courtroom held a certain mystique and air of formality. Flags, portraits of past judges, and slogans proclaiming God's favor adorned the walls. These things prompted all to be respectful and quiet. The gallery accommodated about fifty people, but this morning more than seventy five souls were packed into the small room. Three prosecutors sat at a table in front of and to the left of the elevated judges' bench, and opposite them sat the three-man defense team, and Brooks and Orme. Behind them and on both sides of the room, sat law enforcement, ready to keep order, should order need to be kept.

On the rear wall, an ornate, highly polished clock audibly ticked away the minutes, reminding everyone that patience is a virtue and that some irritations just have to be put up with. At 9:00 am the clock chimed the tones of the hymn 'Rock of Ages,' then fell silent. With that, a door behind the bench opened and Judge Levering, followed closely by Judge DeYoung, entered the courtroom. As the associate judges for this trial, they stood by their seats, waiting respectfully for the President

Judge to enter and occupy the middle and largest chair behind the bench.

They didn't wait long.

"All rise," called the bailiff, and everyone did. George R. Barrett, President Judge of Monroe County made his way, with a purposeful gait, to his seat of authority, and the first murder trial in the history of Monroe County, "William Brooks and Charles Orme vs. the Commonwealth of Pennsylvania," began in the Stroudsburg courthouse.

It didn't take long for boredom to set in, and by mid-morning people in the gallery were shifting and wiggling and changing positions on the hard, oaken benches. Boots scraped against floor boards, throats were cleared and, here and there, whispered conversations broke out like small fires in a dry autumn forest.

Judge Barrett brought his gavel down sharply and the room returned to silence, except for the attorneys who were engaged in a lengthy and litigious discourse that only they and the judges understood.

A glimmer of interest pervaded the room around 11am as the prosecutors and the defense attorneys wrangled over the final selection of jurists. The onlookers perked-up as they watched friends and relatives discarded or selected to serve on the jury.

William Walton, newly hired at the Stroudsburg post office had dutifully carried the many summons to which these men had responded, all anxious to engage in their civic duty and to be part of the proceedings. By 1pm the twelve had been selected, all good, hard-working, honest men who now were sworn to impartiality. Their families had populated Monroe County for generations and would continue to do so. Names like Learn, Doll, Butz, Overfield, Long, Hinton and Miller filled the jury box.

The afternoon session was even more monotonous than the morning. Folks started filtering quietly out of the courthouse. Charles Orme dozed off, the attorneys droned on; the clock ticked away the minutes and hourly chimed the old familiar hymn.

By 3 o'clock, even Judge Barrett had had enough and he signaled, to the bailiff and the tipstaff, his intention to end the session. The Judge understood what lay ahead. The formalities of concluding the proceedings were carried out and soon the room was empty. Brooks and Orme were secured in their cell and a young deputy took up his position outside the jail, prepared to spend another night in the freezing cold.

TRIAL
DAY TWO
29 DECEMBER, 1868

Mr. Troch arrived at the jail at 6am, as he usually did, and began his routine of tending to the wood-burning stove and putting on a pot of coffee. He lit the oil lamps and carried one with him as he went in the back to check on Brooks and Orme, still the only prisoners. Finding them both asleep, he began to sweep the well-worn pine planks of the floor. He shoveled the walk way in front of the jail, then spread some ashes from the stove. He called to the young deputy, who had been standing the night watch, to come in for coffee.

"Morning, Mr. Troch. Sure do thank you for the coffee." His face was beet red with cold.

"You're welcome, son." Mr. Troch called everybody 'son,' except Sheriff Henry.

"You sit here and warm yourself. I'm gonna take coffee back to the prisoners."

With concern in his voice, the young deputy spoke up. "I'll take it, or at least I'll go with you."

"No need. I know they done wrong but they show respect. They call me Mr. Troch. You go on home and get some rest."

The deputies started filtering in around 7am. They huddled around the stove, drinking black coffee and commenting on the previous day's trial. All agreed it was uneventful and boring.

Sheriff Henry and Peter Merwine were the last to arrive, and with coffee cup in hand, Sheriff Henry addressed the deputies.

From behind his desk he said, "You boys done a fine job yesterday. Today's the same procedure. Might be more people around though. I don't expect trouble, mostly 'cause of the way you boys handled yourselves yesterday. Folks kind a give up on the vengeance; just plain old curious now."

He paused and looked down at his desk, then up at the men gathered in the small office of the jail. He swallowed hard before continuing, "Now you men know that come Friday Peter Merwine will be the sheriff." They all knew that. They all knew Peter Merwine had won the election in November. Sheriff Henry declined to run again and had thrown his support behind Merwine. "I expect you boys to treat him with the same cooperation and respect you give me over the past six years. Don't know how long this trial's gonna go on for, but I'm sure it's gonna spill over into next year. I been proud to work with all of ya." The room filled with an awkward silence.

He turned his head to Peter Merwine and nodded and everyone understood the gesture. Starting now their friend and fellow deputy Peter would be addressed as Sheriff Merwine, and the future responsibilities of the office of Sheriff of Monroe County would fall on his shoulders.

They proceeded to the courthouse in the bright morning cold as they had on Monday. The crowd was just as large but without shouts of anger and hatred. The tension-filled air of the day before seemed to have been swept away by the winter wind, and in its place a new perception prevailed. The focus had shifted from the persons of Brooks and Orme, to the trial of Brooks and Orme. The swirl of court proceedings put the judges, the attorneys, and the jury at center stage while Billy and Charlie, their lives hanging on the scales of justice, waited in the wings.

So, the stage was set. Court opened at 10am and the prosecution led. Today's proceedings were interesting and people listened intently.

All eyes turned to Stephan Holmes, the District Attorney, as he rose and called his first witness.

Hannah Brodhead rose and helped her husband Thomas to his feet. Bent and feeble, he steadied himself on the gallery railing before attempting to navigate the fifteen feet to the witness chair. Using a cane, he shuffled slowly for several steps but finally the bailiff came to his aid. Thomas turned to take the oath and the people in the gallery saw him for the first time since he had been beaten and his brother killed. A collective gasp filled the courtroom. People stared in shocked disbelief. Brooks and Orme stared at the floor.

"Are you able to proceed at this time, Mr. Brodhead?" District Attorney Holmes inquired.

Thomas responded by nodding his badly battered head up and down.

President Judge Barrett spoke up. "Thomas, you have to speak your answers. The court reporter has to write down what is said here."

"Yes," Thomas managed, just above a whisper. His right eye was sealed shut and the right side of mouth sagged. Stitches were visible in his shaved scalp and across his forehead. An ugly purple-red line ran from his left eye, down his cheek, and was crisscrossed by black thread - Dr. Jackson's attempt to sew his face back together.

The court reporter slid his chair closer to the witness stand as Thomas began his testimony. He began slowly, struggling to keep his thoughts in order, his voice above a whisper.

"Me and my wife own the Brainerd House. It's in the Water Gap. I was working in a field. Can't remember what I was doing."

"That's fine Thomas. Tell us what happened while you were in the field."

"Two girls that work for me, in the hotel, came running. I could see they was troubled. Said two men just robbed me."

"And do you see those two men in the courtroom, Thomas?"

"Be those two right there." Thomas slowly raised his arm and pointed at Brooks and Orme.

"Very good Thomas. Now, let's continue."

Thomas stared at the District Attorney. "Continue?"

"Yes. You're working in a near-by field. Two of your employees run to you. They tell you the hotel has just been robbed. What do you do then?"

"I went to the hotel, fast as I could. I asked my manager if anybody got hurt. He said no one was hurt, but all the money was gone."

Thomas stared at Brooks and Orme for several seconds.

"Thomas."

"What?"

137

"Tell us what your manager told you."

"He told me what they looked like. He said they didn't have no gun, but they did have a gun." Thomas took the water glass and sipped from it. "And they killed my brother Theodore."

"Alright Thomas, we'll get to that. What did you do after getting a description of the two defendants?"

"I left the hotel and I seen my brother, Theodore, coming out of the post office. I ran to him." Thomas breathed deeply a few times, then continued. "He give me my mail. Picked it up for me. He was considerate like that. Always did kindly by others."

"So you met your brother Theodore at the post office and he gave you your mail?"

"Yes. I told him the hotel had just been robbed and maybe we could catch up with the thieves."

"What did you do with your mail?" The DA would need this information later.

"I put it inside my vest, and, good thing I did." Thomas seemed to be gaining strength.

"Alright Thomas, after the post office, where did you and Theodore go? Remember? You went to the train station." The DA was leading witness but no one seemed to mind and the defense didn't object.

"That's correct. We went to the train station. We

was thinking they might try to leave on the afternoon train, but they hadn't been there."

"How did you know that?"

"Well, Carson said so."

District Attorney Holmes looked up at Judge Barrett, "Your Honor, we ask that the record indicate Thomas is referring to Station Master Carson Wells."

"So ordered."

Thomas again drank from the water glass and seemed to be sitting up straighter.

"Now Thomas, where did you and Theodore go after you left the train station?"

"We walked up the hill to the Kittatinny Hotel."

"Tell us what happened there."

"Talked to my brother William. He's sitting right there." Thomas pointed at William, the proprietor of the Kittatinny and his expression became that of man retreating in time to happier place.

Noting this the DA asked, "Do you want to take some time Thomas?"

"No. I want to tell what them two did," his voice now carried a determined edge. "William said they was there, tried to sell him tools what they stole, so he run 'em off. Told me and Theodore they headed down the old river road, so we out after 'em."

"Very good, Thomas."

Thomas wasn't finished. "William was gonna come with us but we told him no. Told him to stay at the hotel, case they doubled back. They would've killed William too I reckon."

Judge Barrett smiled to himself and waited for the objection that never came. He suggested a brief recess but Thomas said he wanted to continue.

"So your brother William stays at the hotel and you and your brother Theodore continue searching for the two defendants. Tell us about that."

"We walked to the road and sure enough, I seen 'em. Good piece out ahead. Maybe more than a quarter mile. Me and Theodore started walking fast."

"Did you and Theodore reach them at the same time?"

"No. I got to 'em first, but Theodore was real close behind me."

"What happened next Thomas?" DA Holmes asked, his tone gentle but edged with concern. He hoped Thomas could get through reliving the murder of his brother. Thomas looked at Brooks and Orme, everyone else looked at Thomas.

"I said they had my money. I told 'em they had to come with me so as we could get this cleared up." Pointing at Brooks, Thomas stated, "that one said he would, but that one," now pointing at Orme, "said he wouldn't. So I grabbed hold of both of 'em."

Thomas became agitated, his breathing short and quick. He swallowed hard and pulled at the collar of his shirt.

The DA took two steps towards Thomas and spoke in a comforting voice, "You're doing fine Thomas. Let's have a drink of water."

He was surprised by the reply from his star witness. "I don't want water. I want to testify."

"Very well then. You just go ahead and tell us what happened."

Thomas, raising his arm and pointing a shaking hand at Brooks said, "That one picked up the bag with tools in it. He tried to throw it but it hit a rock or a tree, can't rightly remember, but tools and money came out of it."

"Where is Theodore at this point Thomas?"

"That's when he got there."

"And what did he do when he got there?"

"He stood in the middle of the road and said something about the money. Can't recall his exact words. I bent down, started picking up money. Then I heard my brother say 'don't you shoot.' I look up and see that one," again pointing at Brooks, "aiming a gun right at Theodore, so I says, 'you better not shoot.'"

Wanting to paint a clear picture for the jury, the DA asked, "Were you on your hands and knees at this point, Thomas?"

"Yes. And then he shot me. Bullet hit me right here," Thomas put his left hand on the bullet's point of entry. "Felt like a mule kicked me. Bullet hit the mail I was carrying, otherwise would've killed me."

DA Holmes held the bundle of mail, bullet pierced and blood stained, and allowed each member of the jury to examine it. "What happened after you were shot?"

"Then Theodore was shot, shot dead." Thomas' voice trailed off.

"Alright Thomas, take your time. I know how difficult this must be. Were you wounded a second time?"

"Yes. I tried to stand and then that other one," Thomas pointed at Orme, "he took the gun and shot me in the head, but the bullet just grazed me here," and Thomas put his right hand on the right side of his forehead.

"That's all I can recall cause they beat me with a rock or something. Left me laying in the road, thinking I was dead. Next thing I remember I was home, in bed, my wife and Dr. Jackson standing over me."

The courtroom was silent. Everyone still focused on Thomas Brodhead. The more he spoke, the stronger he got. The gallery resisted the urge to break-out in applause. Dr. Jackson, who had been asked to attend in case Thomas collapsed, quietly left the courthouse, now convinced that Thomas would recover.

No one was more pleased than District Attorney Stephan Holmes. He took Thomas Brodhead by the arm and led him back to his seat, confident he would get a conviction of first-degree murder.

When they returned from their lunch recess, the District Attorney went right to work. He presented the bloody shirt Thomas had been wearing, then gave the jury the packet of letters, pierced by a bullet and stained with blood, explaining how the mail had saved the life of Thomas Brodhead. All twelve men in the jury box handled and examined the packet with curiosity and interest.

He concluded his presentation with a large diagram, drawn on blank newspaper, that clearly demonstrated the paths of Brooks and Orme, and of Thomas and Theodore Brodhead. He took special pains to point out the evolution of a planned robbery turning into a premeditated murder.

Court adjourned for the day and the people went back to their everyday lives. Dinners had to be prepared, livestock had to be fed, fires needed to be banked, children needed to work on their lessons, and the Bible had to be read. Brooks and Orme were returned to their cell.

TRIAL
DAY THREE
WEDNESDAY, 30 DECEMBER, 1868

Stephan Holmes glanced around the courtroom, noting that fewer people were in attendance today. He attributed this to the six inches of new snow that had fallen during the night and not to any decrease in interest on the part of local citizens.

He studied the faces of the twelve men in the jury box, looking for telltale signs of sympathy for Brooks and Orme. He detected none and felt sure of a conviction, but his years of experience cautioned him against over confidence. Juries do strange things sometimes.

He turned his attention to the defense table where Brooks and Orme sat, nestled between attorneys

Charlton Burnett, John B. Strom and David S. Lee. He knew them all, knew them well, and knew them capable lawyers. He was slightly puzzled that not one of them had spoken yesterday. No objections had been raised, and his witness, Thomas Brodhead, had not been questioned. He had discussed this with William Davis and Samuel Dreher, the other prosecuting attorneys on his team, and all agreed the silent treatment was a viable strategy, one of few open to the defense team. He mentally reviewed the agenda he and his team had set for today and tried to anticipate everything the defense might say, if in fact, they said anything.

'Rock of Ages' rang out from the back of the courtroom and 'All Rise' sang out from the front.

Throughout the morning and into the early afternoon, the prosecution called witness after witness. Sheriff Henry was called, as was Peter Merwine. Several deputies were called, along with men who had formed the posse. Employees of the Brainerd House and the Kittantinny Hotel were called to the stand. The young reporter, Elliot Kessler, who had thought to use the telegraph, was called. It became monotonous. Everybody knew who murdered Theodore Brodhead. Brooks stared straight ahead, looking contrite, and Orme dozed off. People began to fidget and whisper to each other. The defense team understood. They knew what the District Attorney was doing as he constantly pulled at the heart strings of the jury and continually hammered home the viciousness of the attack on one of their leading citizens.

At 3 o'clock Attorney Holmes called for young Charles Staples, the clerk in the hardware store, who had seen Brooks and Orme steal tools the day before the murder. Mature for his fifteen years, Charles presented himself as a credible witness. And, young Staples felt he had a score to settle. At 3:15pm Theodore's nephew, Edward Brodhead, took the stand. It was into his arms that Thomas collapsed after being beaten beyond recognition. He described, in vivid detail, the horrific appearance of Thomas and the sadness at losing his Uncle Theodore. At 3:30 Edward rose from the witness chair and returned to his seat, surrounded by members of the Brodhead family.

After again surveying the faces of the twelve impaneled jurists, District Attorney Holmes decided it was time for the final blow, the knock-out punch. He called for the Doctor.

Dr. Reeves Jackson strode briskly to the witness box, was duly sworn, and sat down in the chair.

His testimony centered on both Theodore and Thomas. He began with the autopsy of Theodore, leaving no doubt in anyone's mind that he had died from a shot in the chest. He explained that the bullet he removed from Theodore's heart came from the gun that William Brooks had in his possession at the time of his arrest.

Attorney Holmes tried to get Doc Jackson to state that Theodore, a healthy fifty year-old man, would have lived a long and prosperous life had it not been for Brooks and Orme. Reeves Jackson wasn't having any part of that, and he smiled as he informed the court that he was a doctor, not a fortune-teller.

Using layman terms, as he had been coached, Dr. Jackson described the seriousness of the injuries Thomas endured. It was his medical opinion, he concluded, that Thomas would have died had it not been for the mail he carried, and the fact he got medical attention as soon as he did.

All experienced trial lawyers understand 'overkill', and know it should be avoided. The District Attorney turned from the Doctor and looked at the other two prosecutors, attorneys Davis and Dreher. Both were leaning back in their chairs, arms folded on their chests. He turned back to face the President Judge. "I have nothing more, Your Honor."

Before adjourning, Associate Judge DeYoung reminded everyone that court would reconvene the following day, Thursday, December 31st, at 3 o'clock in the afternoon. It was a few minutes before 4 o'clock. It was cold outside and getting dark. People hurried from the courthouse. Nobody wanted to hear 'Rock of Ages' again.

TRIAL
DAY FOUR
THURSDAY, 31 DECEMBER, 1868

The trek to the courthouse was becoming routine, so Sheriff Henry and Sheriff Merwine took a few minutes on this afternoon to remind the deputies that Brooks and Orme were murderers and should not be trusted.

"Stay alert and keep a close watch, men. I don't want any of you getting hurt," Peter Merwine said as he handed his empty coffee cup to old Mr. Troch. "Alright boys, saddle up. Here we go." They marched to the courthouse along the usual route, the hard-packed snow crunching beneath their boots, their breath visible in the bright afternoon cold. Only a few dozen folks were in the street and most of them were just going about their business. From somewhere behind them a male voice boomed, "Good job Sheriff; good job boys."

After the formalities of beginning a court session were seen to, the defense came to life. Their strategy would be to present three points of law that would persuade the jury to return a verdict of something less than first degree murder, hoping to save Brooks and Orme from the hangman's noose. They would not look for pity from this jury and they would not speak to them condescendingly. It had been decided that each of them would take one of the points and explain it convincingly. They would call no witnesses throughout the day, nor would they have the defendants speak. Attorney Charlton Burnett rose, walked to a point near the jury box and began.

As the most experienced and senior member of the team, Attorney Burnett took their strongest point. He looked directly at the jury, focusing on one individual, then another, trying to locate a hint of sympathy, an expression of understanding. He tried to determine who, among these twelve, might be willing to spare the lives of these two young boys. For more than an hour he paced, gesticulated, spoke loudly at times, softly at other times, always eloquently. He had to get them to understand that since no warrant had been issued for their arrest, the arrest of Brooks and Orme had been illegal. He concluded by stating that, in the absence of an arrest warrant, Thomas and Theodore Brodhead, as private citizens, had no right to detain his clients. Consequently, the defendants were not guilty of first degree murder, but manslaughter.

He stood silent for several seconds, surveyed each man on the jury, then thanked them. He returned to his seat at the defense table, determined not to let his disappointment show. A sheet of paper, with the numbers one through twelve on it, lay on the table top, in front of his chair. Each attorney would circle the number of the jurist they felt had shown some inclination in their favor. He made no mark on the paper.

Concerned by that, but determined to provide the murderers with the best possible defense, Attorney John B. Storm, second chair of the three-man team, rose and walked to the jury box. Even though just thirty years old, he was well known, having served admirably as superintendent of schools. He taught Sunday school at the Methodist Church on Main Street and now he would bring his natural teaching abilities to bear on the jury. He picked up the thread left by Charlton Burnett. Not only did the Brodhead brothers not have the right to detain Brooks and Orme, but because Brooks and Orme felt so threatened, and could see no avenue of escape, they had no choice but to fight their way out of the situation. It was simply a tragic accident in which too much force was used, so this is not murder, but manslaughter. He could read it in their faces. Two men in their fifties overcoming two boys in their early twenties, in the open countryside? Well-honed teaching skills are a double-edged sword. Storm knew he had presented the subject material well, but he knew the class wasn't getting it. He politely thanked the men of the jury and returned to his seat. The jury chart remained unmarked.

President Judge George R. Barrett, noting the time to be 6 pm announced a half-hour recess. The jury was ushered to the jury room and given coffee and sandwiches, prepared by the Stroudsburg House; the bill was given to the Mayor, who stared at it in astonishment. The kerosene lamps were lit, and people were moving in and out of the courthouse. Everybody wanted to be there for the verdict but nobody knew when that would be. Charlie Orme proclaimed that he needed to relieve himself, so while that was arranged and accomplished the attorneys huddled at their tables and discussed how things were progressing. The three judges disappeared to their chambers to do whatever it is judges do, and everybody else just sat and waited for 6:30.

The bailiff and the tipstaff put the courtroom back in order and the three judges made their entrance at a little past 6:30pm on the last day of the year and, in the hopes of many, the last day of the trial.

The final point, considered to be the weakest link in the three-point defense strategy, would be presented by the youngest of the three defense attorneys. Attorney David S. Lee was twenty eight years old and had three great loves in his life. First came family, then the law, then baseball. According to his wife, the order was subject to change during the summer months. He was a good-natured young man, had organized the baseball club of Stroudsburg in 1866, and was a talented player. He quietly absorbed the ribbing he still got from friends about his team's 86 to 22 loss to the Neptune Club of Easton, Pa. in the summer of '67.

He stood before the jury, a friendly smile just discernable beneath his flowing handlebar mustache. He had carefully selected his attire, just as he had thoughtfully chosen his words and tone. He spoke to them as one of them, as they would speak to each other. He was confident his point would resonate with at least one member of the jury.

He began with a simplified explanation of the difference between first degree murder and manslaughter. He repeatedly worked in the necessity of 'intent' in order to convict of the more serious charge of murder. Finally, he arrived at the apex of his dissertation. Intent had not been proven. There was no intent because both Brooks and Orme were so drunk that they lacked the mental capacity needed to form intent. He stopped talking, surveyed the faces of twelve men, and said thank-you.

At one point during his presentation, he noticed that juror number three had closed his eyes, a painful expression on his face. Later, he saw juror number seven turn his head, his face flushed. Those two men had done something in drunkenness that they regretted to this day. Attorney Lee was hopeful, and as he returned to the defense table and reached for the jury chart, he heard Charlton Burnett say, "The defense rests, Your Honor." Didn't matter. It was too late to help and he had nothing more to prove. In his heart he knew he had hit a home run.

At 8 pm the District Attorney began the prosecution's closing argument, taking the still attentive jury through the details of the crime and reminding them that their friend and neighbor, Theodore Brodhead, had been intentionally murdered by Brooks and Orme in order to facilitate their escape. At 9:15 pm he turned from the jury, faced the bench and announced with confidence, "Your Honor, the prosecution rests."

A peculiar silence filled the courtroom. Everyone focused their attention on the three judges who were shuffling papers and speaking with each other in hushed tones. No one knew exactly what to do, so they just sat and waited for a judge to say something.

Finally, at 9:30, with the cold winter night wrapped around the tiny courthouse and its window panes coated in ice, President Judge Barrett spoke to the jury.

"Gentlemen, the burden of justice now rests with you. You must deliberate in fairness and impartiality. Take into consideration all the facts as they have been presented and do not allow any personal prejudices to affect your decision. The bailiff will now escort you to the jury room and, if before midnight a decision is reached, you are to inform the bailiff and he will ring the courthouse bell."

CHAPTER V: "SHOOT ME NOW"

TRIAL
DAY FIVE
FRIDAY, JANUARY 1, 1869

With just fifteen minutes left in 1868, the bailiff pulled sharply on the long, heavy rope hanging from the belfry and the tolling of the courthouse bell shattered the frigid night air.

A flurry of activity swirled in and around the courthouse as citizens donned hats and coats and hurriedly made their way up Seventh Street, across the town square and into the courtroom.

Still seated and shackled, and looking more forlorn then ever, Brooks and Orme nervously awaited the outcome of the jury's deliberations.

Their attorneys filtered in and sat next to them, each appearing calm. David S. Lee, the baseball playing lawyer, went so far as to put his hand on Charlie's shoulder, but he spoke no words. The words had all been spoken. It had been spelled out to Billy and Charlie that there was little chance of any outcome other than 'guilty of murder in the first degree.'

That was to be expected here in Stroudsburg. But there was always hope. Juries have been known to do strange things. All three attorneys were confident that the appeals process would reduce that verdict to manslaughter.

A large contingent of Stroudsburg's most local, and most curious, citizens packed themselves into the courtroom, determined to hear the jury announce their verdict first-hand. Sheriff Henry extended his hand to Peter Merwine. "Congratulations Sheriff Merwine." The year 1869 was one hour old, and there was a new sheriff in town. Those deputies seated nearby also whispered their best wishes to Peter Merwine.

The prosecuting attorneys entered and walked confidently to their table, seated themselves, and began planning a luncheon for Sunday at the Indian Queen Hotel. They all agreed the new year should be ushered in with some sort of celebratory event. Dinner with the wives at the Indian Queen Hotel was the unanimous choice.

The menu was extensive, with suckling pig, venison, smoked turkey, and brook trout. The bar was well stocked with imported wines and expensive liquors. A fine selection of cigars awaited the gentlemen. The wives of the attorneys were also anxious to visit the Indian Queen, start of a new year or not. They had heard about the fine furniture, expensive rugs and drapes, and exquisite art work that adorned the walls of the well-appointed dining rooms and salons. They would need their husbands, however, to view these fineries, as ladies were not permitted to enter unless escorted by a gentleman. This enjoyable planning session quickly evaporated when, for the first time in 1869, the bailiff's voice rang through the dimly lit and chilly room.

"All rise."

The three judges emerged from the small room just off the main courtroom and seated themselves at their elevated bench. Without emotion, Associate Judge DeYoung, his face a study in neutrality, instructed the bailiff to "bring in the jury."

THE VERDICT

Though they'd only been gone three and half hours, that time was etched in each man's face. Some appeared slightly disheveled, with shirt tails hanging out and hair uncombed. Some were bleary eyed; none had any spring left in his step. The tiny, cramped room they had just departed was still smoke filled and littered with crumpled pieces of papers. The two windows had been raised in spite of the freezing temperature, and tobacco juice clung, frozen to the west side wall. Attorney Charlton Burnett studied each man as he took his seat in the jury box. Not one man looked at him, or either of his clients. He correctly discerned what he saw; they were united and resolute.

The lack of sleep was taking its toll on everyone, and President Judge Barrett was no exception although he was more successful than most at masquerading his weariness.

He spoke with a clear, even voice, "The defendants will rise." Brooks and Orme and their three man defense team stood. Judge Barrett looked at the twelve ordinary citizens who were now the most important people in Monroe County, and asked, "Gentlemen of the jury, have you reached a unanimous decision?"

Jacob Learn rose and spoke, "We have your Honor." Short, stocky and just north of 50 years of age, he hailed from one of the oldest families in the area. He had a reputation for integrity, was well-liked and, he owned a tavern.

People slid to the edge of their seats.

"Very well. What say you one, what say you all?" Judge Barrett asked of foreman Learn.

Through bleary eyes and without emotion, Jacob read the verdict, prepared and agreed to: *"We the jurors in this case, after giving it clear investigation and consideration, do find the said William Brooks and Charles Orme, charged as the murderers of Theodore Brodhead, to be guilty of murder in the first degree."*

Jacob raised his head and looked at Judge Barrett, who understood and said, "You can sit down now Jacob."

Reactions varied throughout the room, depending on seating.

Smiles were exchanged at the District Attorney's table. At the defense table, William Brooks raised his head, a slight glimmer of defiance in his eyes, while Charles Orme stared at the floor, resignation clearly on his face. Not one of the three defense attorneys showed any disappointment, and they even took time to whisper a few words of hope to the boys seated with them.

The citizens in the gallery murmured in subdued and hushed agreement that was tinged with self-satisfaction and confidence in the system and the people they had elected to run that system. To the observant few it was an indication that Monroe County was moving on. Moving past the shock, the fear and the hatred. Justice and the rule of law had carried the day. The county was coming of age.

President Judge Barrett thanked the jury and announced to the court that they would reconvene on Saturday, January 2 at 10a.m. for the sentencing phase of the trial. He gaveled the session closed and he and the two associate judges exited the room.

Peter Merwine rose, turned to his deputies, and issued his first official command as Sheriff of Monroe County.

"Let's get the hell out of here."

SENTENCING
SATURDAY, JANUARY 2, 1869

By murdering Theodore Brodhead, Brooks and Orme set in motion a series of events that brought together a variety of players who moved from spotlight to shadows on a stage with multiple backdrops. Today would mark the culmination of all the work and preparation of the attorneys, the watchfulness of the judges, and all the diligence of the law enforcement men. A young newspaper reporter and an aging doctor had also played a part in the drama. The citizens of Monroe County were the audience who pushed and shoved, setting manners aside on this Saturday morning in order to get a good seat at what they thought would be the beginning of the final act.

All the players were in their places and at precisely 10a.m. the judges appeared. With bright beams of winter sunlight glaring through dirty window panes and the body heat of more than one hundred souls warming the crowded room, Judge Barrett gaveled the session into order. Understanding that the law and court process were a mystery to most common folks, he explained the procedure to be followed this morning. He accomplished this by directing his instructions towards both groups of attorneys.

Judge Barrett shifted slightly in his chair, picked up the piece of paper in front of him and began. "It is the intention of this court that before passing sentence on both William Brooks and Charles Orme that they be allowed to make statements. They should be brief and to the point." He knew they would be because he had instructed their attorneys that they would be. "At the conclusion of their statements, I will read their sentences. William Brooks will be sentenced first, then Charles Orme. At that point, this trial will be concluded. William Brooks, rise and address the court."

Billy rose and spoke as his defense team had coached him. He did his best to sound sincere, refrained from legalistic terms, not that he knew any, and went so far as to say he felt bad that Mr. Brodhead had died. He fixed his gaze on Judge Barrett and kept it there throughout his monologue. He did not deny his guilt but he emphasized that there was no premeditation and certainly no malicious intent. Done, he just sat down.

"Charles Orme, rise and address the court." Though not a monotone, there was no emotion in the voice of President Judge George R. Barrett.

Charlie got up and steadied himself against the table. He said good morning to the judge and then pretty much reiterated what Billy had said. He wasn't as good at speaking as Billy and stumbled here and there, but he did come across as more sincere and truly sorry for the death of Theodore. He thanked the court then sat down heavily in his chair.

The defense team thought the boys had done a good job presenting themselves and felt the 'no premeditation' statement carried a little weight. The 'no malicious intent' clause fell flat and all three lawyers realized, too late, that it should not have been used.

Judge Barrett again repositioned himself in his large but uncomfortable chair, picked-up a different sheet of paper and began a summary of the crime, recapping the details of September 25, 1868 and telling Brooks and Orme that they did, in fact, act with malicious intent. Attorney Charlton Burnett felt the sting of that not very subtle rebuke.

"The court will now pass sentence on William Brooks."

Billy stood, as did Charlton Burnett, John B. Storm, and David S. Lee.

Judge Barrett cleared his throat and began: *"There is but one thing for you to do in this your hour of extremity. Go back to your cell and engage in secret, earnest and devout prayer to Almighty God. He alone can grant you the pardon you most need; with him there is hope even for you. Read and study your Bible; confess your sins to Him and Him alone. When you leave this world, you must enter upon eternity! This life is at best but a brief period; Eternity is unending. It only remains for us to pass upon you the sentence of the Law, which is: That you, William Brooks, be taken to the jail of Monroe County from whence you came, and from thence to the place within the walls or yard of said jail, and there be hanged by the neck until you are dead. And may God have mercy on your soul."*

Billy sat, Charlie stood, Judge Barrett read again and the young reporter scribbled every word in his notebook.

Having passed identical sentences on both murderers, Judge Barrett gaveled the trial to an end, and the three judges stood up in unison and left the courtroom.

Six days after it began, it ended, as most people expected it would. What had not been anticipated was the reaction of the people sitting in the courtroom. No outbursts of joy, no shouting, no clapping, no cheering, broke the silence. People got up, adjusted their coats and scarves, and pulled gloves back onto their chapped, calloused hands. They conversed little and when they did they spoke in hushed tones as if they were in church. With the room empty of citizens, Sheriff Merwine directed his deputies to escort Brooks and Orme back to the jail. As they departed, the opposing teams of lawyers met in the middle of the room, shook hands and commended each other on their legal maneuverings, then departed for the Indian Queen.

The bailiff and the tipstaff, friends and co-workers for many years, walked through the deserted room, checking for personal items left behind. They closed and locked the courtroom door, walked together down the hall and exited the courthouse.

It was 12 noon, and 'Rock of Ages' played to an empty house.

THE GOVERNOR'S MANSION
HARRISBURG, PA.
MONDAY, FEBRUARY 1, 1869

A bitter cold wind blew along the Susquehanna River and invaded every room in the Governor's Mansion with bone-chilling drafts. Members of the domestic staff scurried from room to room battening windows, closing curtains and, depending on the heat source, adding wood or coal, to already blazing fires. The heat of the kitchen beckoned all staff members to its warm embrace, even those that didn't know how to boil water, until, in exasperation, the executive chef threw them all out.

The Governor liked his breakfast served in his study at 9a.m. At that hour an attractive, young woman in a starched white apron, gloves and a bonnet, knocked on his door and waited for John White Geary, the sixteenth Governor of Pennsylvania, to call out, as he always did, "Enter," a habit from his years of military service. He had fought heroically during the Civil War, was breveted to Major General, and had been wounded five times. At six foot six inches tall and 260 pounds, he had been a hell of a target.

The breakfast tray held hot, black coffee, two freshly baked muffins, a rasher of bacon, two fried eggs, and the morning paper, *The Harrisburg Telegraph*. The girl smiled politely and retreated to the warmth of the basement kitchen. The Governor devoured the food and the news quickly, and then set himself to his work. He was not a man to procrastinate and there was pressing business to attend to.

From the top of the pile of papers on the left side of his large, mahogany desk, he retrieved the neatly bound file marked 'death warrants,' and began reading thoughtfully. He had been briefed about the case against Brooks and Orme, knew the verdict and the sentence, but was not about to send two young men to the gallows without a thorough review of the proceedings. He read slowly and carefully, beginning with a transcript of the trial and working his way through to several newspaper accounts of the crime, discarding one from the Philadelphia Inquirer, which he thought prejudicial, not to mention poorly written.

By 11a.m., with the wind subsiding and the curtains opened, he finished reading, closed the 'death warrant' file and walked to the windows that looked out on Front Street and the ice choked Susquehanna River. Bitterly he remembered holding his son as the boy died from his wounds at the Battle of Wauhatchie in eastern Tennessee. His son, Edward, would be about the same age as the two murderers, whose lives he now held in his hands. He returned to his desk and summoned his most senior aide who quickly appeared at the study door with a shawl draped over his shoulders.

"Are you cold, Robert?" The Governor enjoyed little jokes.

"Yes, General, I am very cold." Those who had been with John White Geary a long time, like Robert, still addressed him as General.

"Come and sit by the fire if you like," the Governor said invitingly, then continued in a more governor-like tone. "I find no breech of proper legal proceedings in any of this." He picked up the folder then let it fall to the desk top. "Nor do I find anything that could be considered a violation of any constitutional rights afforded the accused. And, for the life of me, I can find no reason for clemency." He lowered himself into his chair and exhaled audibly. He looked across his desk at Robert, who nodded in agreement, and he felt better. Robert didn't always agree.

"I am, however, troubled by their ages. One of them is 25, and the other is only 22." The old General sounded exasperated and confounded at the same time. Robert maintained his silence. Having been aide-de-camp to General Geary throughout the war, he understood the battle that was being fought in the heart of the man seated behind the desk.

The Governor removed his rimless spectacles and rubbed his eyes, then continued. "Do we know how the folks in Monroe County feel?"

Robert sat back in his chair then spoke with an air of certainty. "Our friends up there tell me that if you don't sign, we'll have some explaining to do before the next election. If the Supreme Court reduces the sentence to life in prison, should the appeal get that far, we can use that to our advantage in the next campaign."

"Very well then. I'm signing both execution warrants, now, and setting the date of execution for the twenty sixth of this month. That should give them enough time to get their appeals in order, or build the gallows, and I'm washing my political hands of this entire situation. You know Robert, those ol' boys up there didn't vote for Lincoln."

"I know that Governor, but they did vote for you."

THE APPEAL

Thieves, murderers, accused prisoners, condemned men. Billy and Charlie were progressing nicely through the levels of criminality. With their execution date looming on the horizon, the defense team sprang into action and filed the necessary paperwork to start the appeals process, which would, if nothing else, at least delay the date of execution.

The appeal eventually did reach the Pennsylvania Supreme Court. It was straight-forward, and encapsulated the three arguments brought out at the trial in Stroudsburg.

First: The arrest of Brooks and Orme was illegal because no arrest warrant had been issued and private citizens, the Brodhead brothers, had no right to detain them.

Second: Brooks and Orme, surrounded and feeling threatened, had no choice but to fight their way out.

Third: Both boys were too drunk to form any thought of premeditation or malicious intent.

Consequently, they were guilty of manslaughter, not first degree murder.

The Supreme Court of the great state of Pennsylvania put the case on their docket for Wednesday, March 31, 1869, and on that date the seven Justices convened and, after due deliberation, upheld the ruling of the lower court. Billy and Charlie were, indeed, to die for the murder of Theodore Brodhead.

The news reached Stroudsburg the next day and, with the exception of Brooks and Orme, was well received.

Little had changed in their existence since January. They had been provided with an extra blanket, but were still cold; the food remained bland and Charlie remained hungry. Once a week they were given a newspaper. They were watched, day and night, but never engaged in conversation with the deputies, even though Billy tried. Old Mr. Troch spoke with them when he brought the meals to their cell but he was always accompanied by a deputy who limited the talking. They didn't know that he had asked Sheriff Merwine if he could set up a checkerboard outside the cell and play checkers with them. The request was immediately denied. Sheriff Peter Merwine ran a very tight ship.

ᘓᘓᘓ

Spring arrived like a freight train on Thursday morning, the first day of April, 1869. Sheriff

Merwine left his house and walked down Main Street, pinning his badge to his vest as he walked by the American House Hotel on the corner at Eighth Street. The early morning sun spilled its way up the muddy street, coaxing crocuses from their winter sleep. He contemplated the task that awaited him at the jail. In his mind he went over the words he would use to inform Brooks and Orme, officially, that their appeal had been denied and that they would be executed.

He arrived at the jail just as the church bell began to announce that it was 7a.m., and found that the reliable Mr. Troch had already made coffee and was busily sweeping up around his desk.

"Morning Mr. Troch."

"Morning Sheriff."

"Are they awake?" he inquired of the old man.

"Yes, they are, son. Sorry, I mean Sheriff," apologized Mr. Troch.

Peter Merwine smiled. That was not the kind of thing that bothered him.

"Alright, let's get this over with. I'll need a deputy for a witness." Just a hint of resignation rose in Sheriff Merwine's voice.

"That young Robert Jenkins is outside. He stood the night watch. Want me to call him in?" asked Mr. Troch.

Before Sheriff Merwine could answer, the door swung open and a bleary-eyed Deputy Jenkins entered the jail office. Tired, but smiling with youthful exuberance, he said good morning to the sheriff, to Mr. Troch, and headed for the coffee pot.

"Hold on for a minute, Deputy. I have to talk to the prisoners and I want you to be present while I do." Robert Jenkins was new to the department but he understood what he was about to witness.

◑◑◑

It had been an exhausting day for Sheriff Merwine. By mid-afternoon he had a pounding headache. The small disturbances he usually overlooked were getting the best of him. He was glad he was going to meet Sheriff Henry at the bar of the Stroudsburg House, and 5p.m. couldn't come soon enough for him today.

The retired Sheriff arrived first because he was retired and had no pressing duties. He was robustly greeted by old friends, and without even asking, a glass of beer arrived at his table.

"That's on me, Sheriff," called the mustachioed bartender, grinning broadly. He had enjoyed

173

playing the part of the murderer, Billy Brooks, back in December as they rehearsed walking the prisoners to the courthouse.

Sheriff Henry raised his glass in gratitude and drank from it.

He had just finished his beer when Sheriff Merwine arrived, and the bartender, jovial as always, sent a beer and the same greeting to Peter.

They settled back in the hard, wooden chairs, and Sheriff Henry opened.

"You tell 'em this morning?"

"Sure did, first thing. Had that new kid as witness." Sheriff Merwine answered.

"Well, how'd they take it?" The retired sheriff leaned forward and put his elbows on the table.

"Pretty much like you'd expect. Didn't thank me. Orme sat down and put his head in his hands but Brooks says, 'when?'. I told him I didn't know for certain, but soon." Peter remained in his relaxed position. " I don't like that kid. He's a cocky little bastard."

Two more beers arrived, this time with the expectation of payment.

"Any of their lawyers come calling today?" Sheriff Henry knew the answer.

"Not a one." Both men laughed out loud and drank their beer.

BREAKOUT

The dying embers of hope, never much of a blaze to begin with, were rekindled now by the winds of desperation. When not under the direct observation of a deputy, Billy and Charlie huddled together and, in whispers, Billy informed Charlie of his plan to get them out of jail, out of town, and free of the hangman's noose. All day Friday Billy drilled Charlie on the details, questioning and reminding him of what to say and how to act. He needed to be sure Charlie understood his role, thus ensuring a successful escape on the evening of Saturday, April, 3. This time he needed Charlie. Billy Brooks had no intention of dying at the age of 22.

"Charlie, Charlie. Wake-up." Billy whispered urgently as he pushed on Charlie's shoulder. "Let's go. We're getting out of here. Old man Troch's staying in the jail tonight." The church bell tolled midnight.

"What the hell?" Charlie rubbed his eyes awake. "What's going on?"

"Not sure," Billy whispered. "Heard something about that new deputy had to leave and old man Troch's coming to stay in the jail overnight. Get your fat ass up and get ready. We'll use the old man instead of the young deputy. That's even better."

"I ain't hurting Mr. Troch." Charlie said in a hushed but emphatic voice.

"You're going to do just what I told you. When that church bell rings three times, we're making our move." Billy was more emphatic.

Billy lay down on the floor, in the middle of the cell, and Charlie, standing by the cell door, called out for the old jail janitor, trying to sound distressed.

"Mr. Troch, Mr. Troch. Come quick, something wrong back here with Billy."

When Mr. Troch arrived at the cell, kerosene lamp in hand, Billy was on the floor writhing and making gurgling sounds.

"I think he be having some kind a fit or something. Can you help him Mr. Troch?" Charlie was playing his part well, so was Billy.

"Alright, son." Mr. Troch unlocked the door and stepped into the cell. "Let's get him up on the cot," and he reached down to take hold of Billy's arms.

At that moment, Billy's arms reached up and firmly took hold of Mr. Troch. Billy roughly swung the old man around and threw him on the cot, banging his balding head on the rough stone wall.

Dim light and kerosene fumes filled the tiny cell and William Brooks stared menacingly into the face of a very frightened Mr. Troch. "You stay put old man or I'll kill ya!" Unable to face Mr. Troch, Charles Orme looked away.

"Let's go, Charlie."

Billy raced out of the cell first. Charlie scrambled through the door, pushed it shut and turned the key in the lock. He took a darting glance at Mr. Troch, who sat dazed and in pain on the small cot. Charlie felt ashamed of himself, but he didn't want to die.

Mr. Troch sat for several seconds, collecting himself and listening intently to the sound of fleeing footsteps. He knew in what direction they were heading. He took his handkerchief from the pocket of his tattered, wool jacket and held it against the back of his head. He was bleeding but not badly. He took a couple of deep breaths, tried to stand but was too dizzy. More deep breaths, another attempt, and he was upright. He tottered his way to the front of the cell, reached through the bars and unlocked the door with the key Charlie had forgotten to take.

He bent over to pick up his lamp and his knees buckled. He stayed down on all fours, breathing deeply, feeling strength slowly return on the strong wings of determination. He navigated his way back to the office area and reached up to pull the rope that would sound the alarm bell. He knew the bell would ring, loud and clear. He knew the rope would not break and that the clapper was rust free and well oiled. It was his job to maintain it. He obviously was not a great jailer, but he was one hell of a janitor.

The vengeance, once thought gone, returned now, just before dawn, with the force of a hurricane. Every able-bodied man within the sound of the alarm bell turned out. Some were on foot, others on horseback. All were armed and all were angry.

Concerned for old man Troch, Sheriff Merwine sent for Dr. Jackson while the outraged citizens gathered in front of the jail. There was no need of explaining. The clanging of the bell meant one thing. Brooks and Orme had escaped. Shouting to be heard over the din of the mob, with his deputies gathered near him, Sheriff Merwine loudly proclaimed, "There'll be a $1000 reward for the man that brings them back. And that means alive. No money is gonna be paid for a dead carcass. I'm hanging those two sons-a-bitches myself." And the citizens roared their approval.

Sheriff Henry stood across the street. The flickering glow of a street lamp cast long shadows in the early morning darkness. He watched in concerned silence as his successor took charge, commanding and directing those who would now make every effort to recapture the two murderers. Mob rule is a dangerous thing he thought, as he pushed his way across the street through the crowd. He met up with Doc Jackson and together they went to check on Mr. Troch. The roughing up of that old man pissed him off.

They had run south, just as Mr. Troch said they had. When they got to the McMichaels Creek, they turned east and waded in the cold shallow water close by the edge, trying not to leave obvious footprints.

"Charlie," Billy spoke softly, but urgently, "throw the keys out in the middle of the creek."

"What keys?"

In that moment, Billy made a decision he'd been thinking about for a long time.

The sky lightened with the rising sun, but never cleared. Dark, heavy clouds covered the ridge-line near the river and a light, misty rain began to fall. By mid-morning they were only about five miles away from the jail. Billy kept up a pace difficult for Charlie, but by noon, the boys arrived in the area just north of a place known to locals as the Minisink.

They ran to a stand of pines to get out of the rain and Charlie fell to the ground, breathing heavily. "I can't go no further, Billy."

"We'll stay here, just a couple minutes." Billy too was breathing rapidly. "I'm going up to the top of that knoll just ahead. See if I can spot a barn or something we can hole-up in. Soon as I find something, I'll double back for you. You stay put, now, ya hear?"

Billy got to the top of the knoll and turned to see if Charlie was still hunkered down in the pines. He raced down the far side of the embankment, slipping and sliding in wet grass and deepening mud. Through the sycamore trees and budding oaks, he could see the Delaware River. He kept it on his right as he ran, northward, stumbling through the dense undergrowth. Charles Orme, wet and cold from the early spring rain, rested in the pines. He never saw William Brooks again.

Cold, wet and miserable as he was, Charlie slept all night from exhaustion. The storm retreated to the Jersey side of the Delaware River and Charlie woke on Sunday morning to the springtime sound of birds and soft, early morning light filtering through the pine boughs. He felt a sharp, jarring pain in his left foot and expected it was Billy, returned to lead him off to safety. He opened his eyes to disaster. Five men stood in a semi-circle in front of him. They were all armed and they were all smiling.

In seconds he went from startled to resigned. He sat up and said, "shoot me. Just shoot me now."

"Shit, nobody's gonna shoot you boy," the tallest man in the center of the group said, still smiling. "You ain't worth shit dead."

"You're worth good money alive. Be stupid to kill ya, even though I would like to," said the shortest man in the group, who wasn't smiling.

"Yeah, god-damn good money, too. Be even better if'n they was payin' by the pound." Everybody except Charlie laughed and the man who had made the joke walked toward Charlie. He tied Charlie's hands behind his back and shoved him forward roughly. "Get walking. You're goin' back to jail, son. There's a man with a rope waiting for ya."

Charles Orme was returned to his cell. Mr. Troch returned to his day-time schedule. Sheriff Merwine doled out the reward money to the deserving men and many gallons of beer flowed across the bars of local establishments. No one seemed to notice the underlying current of apprehension concerning the execution of young Mr. Orme. No one except Dr. Reeves Jackson.

Each morning, for a week, Mr. Troch carried a cup of coffee and some stale biscuits back to Charlie's cell. The boy turned away and refused to take the small breakfast or even acknowledge the old janitor. Finally, Mr. Troch spoke. "Alright now, son. Bygones is bygones. I know you ain't bad in your heart. Not like that other one. Now you take this coffee and biscuit."

"I'm truly sorry you was hurt, Mr. Troch," Charlie said, with sincerity, and he reached for the meager meal.

"I know that, son. I don't think you'd be in this fix if it weren't for that scoundrel, Billy Brooks. God knows you ain't no good at it. Leaving the keys in a cell door you're trying to lock a person in."

Charlie smiled for the first time since September of last year.

BILLY'S DEAD?

Word of the capture of Billy Brooks on May 12, spread quickly through the little town of Stroudsburg. There were as many versions of the story as there were people telling it. Sheriff Merwine instructed his people to refrain from discussing the incident until he read through the lengthy report he had just received from the sheriff in Milford, a small town about thirty miles north of Stroudsburg. The Milford sheriff related how a certain Pierre Laurent, who apprehended deserters for the Union Army during the Civil War, spotted

Brooks wandering around in the woods, became suspicious and took him into custody.

He finished the report and laid it on his desk. He made a mental note to send the Milford Sheriff a letter of thanks and he decided to inform Charles Orme of the details of the capture of Billy Brooks, but he'd do that tomorrow.

ლლლ

He took a couple sips of coffee, glanced at the early morning police reports, than looked at Mr. Troch and said, "I'll be in the back, speaking to the prisoner. Anyone comes in, you keep 'em here, in the office. Deputies included."

"Yes Sheriff." Old Mr. Troch went back to sweeping as the sheriff made his way to the cell area.

"Charles Orme, step forward." Peter Merwine could be formal when he felt the situation warranted formality.

Still dejected over being deserted by his only friend, Charlie turned slowly from the small window on the back wall and shuffled the few steps to the bars of the cell door.

"Yes Sheriff?"

"I've thought this over and I believe you deserve to know the facts about the capture of William Brooks."

"Billy's caught?" Charlie stared expectantly at the sheriff.

"Seems he was taken into custody by a French tracker, about thirty miles due north of here. On their way to the jail in Milford, Brooks attempted to escape from the man by jumping off a 30-foot cliff. Several men searched for two days but never could locate him. Feeling is, he crawled in a cave and died, or else he drowned and his body sank down in the swamp. It's pretty much certain he's dead."

"Billy's dead?" Charlie's voice was just above a whisper.

Sheriff Merwine turned and went back to his desk. Charles Orme leaned on the cell door.

SURVIVAL

Billy Brooks survived the fall and no one was more surprised than Billy Brooks. But, he was injured. Both ankles were terribly swollen and he was sure his left wrist and collar bone were broken. His face and hands were a collection of deep, bleeding cuts. He crawled in a cave and stayed in it for three days, unable to move, trying to clear his mind of thirst, hunger and pain. On the fourth day he crawled to the front of the cave and, seeing daylight, crawled back, waiting for the cover of darkness. After several hours he emerged from the mouth of the cave and, dragging himself along by his elbows, managed to find a spring by the light of a half moon. He drank cold water from his cupped hand until his thirst was quenched, then removed his boots and plunged his feet and ankles into the pool. He almost cried out in agony. He stayed out most of the night, gaining strength from the fresh air and taking note of his surroundings. He crawled back into the cave at first light and slept all day.

He repeated this nightly ritual for a week, recuperating by eating may-apples and mushrooms and soaking in the stream. He was young and strong and his vitality returned to him quickly. The swelling in his ankles subsided and when he was finally able to get back into his boots, he decided it was time to move on. As the sun began to set, he began walking towards it. He walked at night, slept during the day. In the gathering twilight of the first day he came to a stand of pines and noticed a small lean-to shack in a clearing about one hundred yards below. He thought about going down and asking for food, but instinct told him to keep moving. It was a good thing he did, because Pierre Laurent didn't like being foiled.

ALONE

Summer on the Pocono Plateau is a delightful time and this summer of 1869 was no exception. Hot summer days were followed by comfortable starlit nights. Flowers bloomed, mountain laurel blossomed, and ripening fruits scented the air. Stroudsburg bustled with the activity of business, social and church life. Children played and laughed in the dusty streets, and young adults danced and sang while engaging in the rituals of courtship.

Charles Orme didn't really feel June passing. He existed in that nether world where things are seen but not engaged. Where joy exists but is not partaken. Where sadness does not touch the immune human heart. Where one is only partially alive, simply because one is not completely dead. Where nothingness is everything and nothing means anything. The sun rose and set thirty times, June bowed to July and Charles Orme sat, alone, in the Stroudsburg jail.

THE GOVERNOR'S MANSION
HARRISBURG, PA.
THURSDAY, JULY 1, 1869.

Governor Geary was not a man who let his anger show but when he became annoyed it was obvious he was annoyed and today he was annoyed.

It was hot as hell and the humidity in the state capitol put everyone on edge. All the doors and windows in the Governor's Mansion had been opened, but nothing alleviated the discomfort of no breeze. It did, however, allow hordes of flies and mosquitoes to enter the Governor's domain.

"Robert." The Governor called out for his senior aide, who quickly appeared at the open office door, without a jacket, shirt unbuttoned at the neck and his sleeves rolled-up.

"Are you warm, Robert?" The Governor like to point out the obvious.

"Yes sir, I am. What can I do?" Robert responded while mopping his forehead with a white handkerchief.

"I got two more execution warrants here. One for Brooks. One for Orme. What the hell's going on up there in Stroudsburg? I thought Brooks was dead." His annoyance was starting to show.

"They think Brooks is dead, but just in case he isn't dead, and if they manage to recapture him, they want to make him dead." Robert had a sense of humor.

"What about the other one?" the Governor asked, even more annoyed.

"They want to make him dead too." Robert was actually enjoying this.

The Governor picked up the warrants and held them out to Robert. "Here, I've signed them both, again. The date is set for Wednesday, August 11. Maybe somebody will show up this time." Robert reached for the documents as the old General continued, "And make it clear to those boys up there that if they don't hang somebody on August 11, I'm commuting the sentence.

Robert turned and went back to his desk while the sixteenth Governor of the great state of Pennsylvania went back to fanning himself.

CHAPTER VI:
LET'S GET THIS
THING BEHIND US

MONDAY MORNING – JULY 12, 1869

Heat lightning and thunder forced him from his bed at 4a.m.; by 6a.m. Sheriff Merwine was at his desk, reading through routine court documents and reports from his deputies. But his mind was focused on a larger issue.

He was in uncharted water. There was no precedent to follow, no star to steer by. He drew his own chart based on what he felt was right. He had faith in his own judgment but prepared himself for the criticism he knew would flow.

Mr. Troch, fully recovered from the escape attempt, arrived just before seven and began his usual duties, which started with making and taking coffee back to the cell of Charlie Orme. He was unaware, however, that just ten minutes ago, Sheriff Merwine had informed Orme, without a witness, that his execution was scheduled for August 11, thirty days hence.

"Mr. Troch." The old man stopped, shifted the hot tin cup from one hand to the other and looked at the sheriff but didn't speak.

"I been doing some thinking. You want to play checkers with Orme now and then, that'll be alright by me." Sheriff Merwine went back to reading reports. He was reluctant to tell Troch the worst.

"Thank you, Sheriff. I thank you, and so does Charlie." Mr. Troch delivered the coffee and the good news, unaware of the bad news delivered earlier.

By 7:30a.m. all the deputies were present and accounted for. The tiny jail house office was crowded with men in badges and uniforms, eager for the regular Monday morning meeting to begin. Sheriff Merwine looked up at the cluster of deputies in their usual positions: senior deputies near the front, closest to his desk and the coffee and biscuits, junior deputies in the rear, leaning against the wall. Mr. Troch, typically on hand, was still in the back, at the cell of Charles Orme.

"Morning Gentlemen," he began, looking up but not smiling. "I have been informed that the execution of Charles Orme is scheduled for August 11, thirty days from today." He continued in an even tone. "In accordance with the law, and the sentence as ordered by Judge Barrett, the execution must take place within the walls or yard of this jail. As you know, this jail has no yard." Something resembling laughter began, but quickly dissolved as the unsmiling sheriff continued. "So, we will hang the condemned man inside the walls of this jail."

Although they all thought it, only the most senior deputy said it out loud: "How in the holy hell we gonna do that?"

"Those particulars will be worked out between now and August 11. In the meantime, you men will see to your regular duties. And there will be some additional assignments and changes over the next month." He had their attention now. Nobody wanted any additional assignments, and everybody hated changes, but the sheriff had made up his mind. He would do what he thought was right.

Before he could continue, the senior deputy spoke up again. "When you gonna be telling us about this new shit?"

"Just as soon as you quit interrupting me." Nervous laughter arose but fell flat.

Peter Merwine was never heavy-handed with the men, nor was he ever dictatorial. He gave orders in a calm, even voice, expecting them to be carried out. On the rare occasions when expectations were not met, he took the underperformer aside and corrected him, counseling rather than reprimanding. He spoke in that manner this morning.

"In the days to come, you will see Mr. Troch playing checkers with Charles Orme – with my permission. They have my permission, no one else. You will soon notice an increase in the quantity, and perhaps quality, of food brought here for the prisoner. I'll be speaking with our friends at the Stroudsburg House later today about that. And I'll be ordering a new cot and mattress that will arrive soon."

They sat and stared in silence. So far, so good, but they knew more was coming.

"Two ministers have requested permission to visit, on a weekly basis, and I have agreed to that. They will need to be accompanied by a deputy.

"On Sunday afternoons, starting this week and continuing up to the week of the execution, prisoner Orme will be allowed out of his cell, and out of the jail, from 1p.m. until 4p.m. He will remain handcuffed; two deputies will be with him during those hours." The sheriff paused for a second, letting all this sink in. He lowered his voice and continued. "We will need a burial detail. The grave will need to be dug and filled, no stone or marker will be placed on it however. I am looking for men to volunteer for these additional assignments – for extra pay in their envelopes, of course. If you're interested, see your shift captain. If not, I'll draw names." Still standing behind his desk, he looked around the room, waiting for someone to speak. He gave them an opening. "Questions?"

Several deputies started at once, so he pointed to one of the younger ones in the back of the room who asked, with some concern in his voice, "When we have the prisoner outside, where do we take him?" All eyes turned back to the sheriff. That seemed to be the question they all had.

He began slowly. "I'm going to be honest. I haven't thought that through yet. Not far, maybe over to the square and back." He would have welcomed suggestions but decided not to ask for them just yet. Though this needed to play out a little more, he was still convinced he was doing the right thing.

From the middle of the group another deputy spoke up. "I ain't opposed to letting him have some fresh air and sunshine, but he don't need three hours of it." That comment garnered the murmured approval of the group.

"Good point. I'll cut it back, maybe one hour," the sheriff conceded.

One of the shift captains stood to make his point. "I ain't opposed to your way of thinking here Sheriff, but maybe you got the wrong day in mind. Stroudsburg Band gonna be playing in the square on Sunday afternoons. Folks come out to hear them, plus all them church people will be walking around. Maybe Saturday be better." Again came the sound of group approval as the shift captain took his seat.

Peter Merwine wasn't backing off on this part. "Sunday crowds always well-behaved folks. Saturday crowds can get rowdy as hell. You men

John H. Abel

know that." The sound of agreement was pronounced. "Besides, folks come out to listen to the band. They probably won't even notice." The tension broke and everyone laughed at that statement, even Sheriff Merwine.

It wasn't caused by the orders of the Sheriff. It had more to do with an inherent kindness of the human heart. Long, hot summer days seemed to have melted away the cold-heartedness of the past winter. Yes, Charles Orme was a convicted murderer. Yes, he had killed one of their own, one of their most respected, and best liked. But the softening had begun.

Ministers became regular visitors. Reverend Pearce from the Presbyterian Church in Delaware Water Gap spent an hour with Charlie on Wednesday afternoons. On Saturday mornings he was counseled by Reverend Ridgway from the Stroudsburg Methodist Episcopal Church. To their surprise, they encountered a young man resigned to his fate and determined to make, during his final days, a contribution to others.

When Orme requested paper and pencil, Mr. Troch relayed that request to Sheriff Merwine who saw to it that paper and pencil were provided. When not engaged in games of checkers, Charles wrote. He wrote everyday and into the evening, as long as he had enough light. He was, however, secretive with the pages and not even Mr. Troch knew what had been written.

Oddly enough, Sheriff Merwine had been right about Sunday strollers taking no notice of Charlie and two deputies. On the Sunday before the execution, the trio stepped out of the jail to the strains of "Lorena" played by the Stroudsburg Band. As they walked to an area out-of-sight, behind the Stroudsburg House, Charlie mentioned how much he enjoyed that song which he'd heard over in the Gap last fall. The deputies stared at each other in silence, their Gap recollection of last fall, a dirge of death. They took Charlie back to his cell where he resumed his writing.

MONDAY AFTERNOON – AUGUST 9, 1869

"Don't want to disturb you, Sheriff," whispered retired Sheriff Henry, after knocking. He stood, silhouetted in the door way of the town jail and continued. "The way you got the door propped open, I thought you might be looking for company."

"You're always welcomed here, Sheriff. Take a seat. Been wanting to talk with you anyway," said Sheriff Merwine. The door had been propped open because it was a hot, humid mid-summer afternoon. They eye-balled each other across the desk that once belonged to Sheriff Henry, now the domain of Sheriff Merwine. Mutual respect and admiration filled the tiny office.

Sheriff Henry went first. "That was a good idea you had, asking them boys from Easton to come up here and stay over Saturday night, share their experience with us. I thank you for letting me sit in on that."

"Wouldn't have done that without you being present," Sheriff Merwine said honestly. "Herman, the Chief of Police down there in Easton, he showed just how to tie the knot so as to get a quick neck snap. There's a lot to it, more than you might think."

Sheriff Henry stared across the desk in concentrated silence, then he spoke. "I'm sure there's a knack to it."

Peter Merwine couldn't help smiling as he said, "Noticed you were getting on pretty good with his brother, Ezra Bachman, the warden down there. They got themselves a big, modern jail I understand." Charles Henry and Ezra Bachman had become fast friends that Saturday. The bartenders at the Stroudsburg House had been busy pulling beers for them well into Sunday morning.

Not a man to make apologies for past behavior, Sheriff Henry replied, "Sure do owe Ezra a debt of gratitude. You know he sent me a letter last year, when I was sheriff, warning me about Brooks and

Orme. Said they was bad, and he was right. He's a good man." He took a blue and white handkerchief from inside his coat and mopped his forehead, then continued. "Now don't misunderstand. I'm not here to meddle, I'm here to help."

"I know that, and I appreciate it." Sheriff Merwine smiled and sat back in his chair, waiting for Sheriff Henry to start meddling.

"I hear tell your planning to hang this boy inside the jail." Sheriff Henry asked, trying to sound nonchalant.

"Got to do what the law says." Sheriff Merwine replied.

"I remember, just a little while back, I was walking down Ninth Street, and I run into Valentine Kautz. The man's a master carpenter, and he told me that when he lived in Bavaria, he and his father built a couple of gallows. Maybe you ought to go see him. Hire him to build the contraption. You know, so it's done right." Sheriff Henry sat back and reached for his handkerchief again.

"Ain't that the damnedest thing. Mr. Kautz is bringing the lumber in later today and he's gonna start building tomorrow morning," Peter Merwine replied with feigned astonishment. He knew that Charles Henry had spoken to old man Kautz last week, after he had already hired him. "Too bad we gotta build it in sight of the condemned."

Sheriff Henry didn't seem bothered by that observation and continued with his concerns. "What about space? Did you tell Kautz that ceiling is only fifteen feet high?"

"Yes, I did and I was assured by Mr. Kautz that would be sufficient." Although always respectful of the senior sheriff, Peter Merwine found himself wishing he could say something that would bring the meeting to an end. "You want a cup of coffee, Sheriff?"

"No. Too hot for coffee. Speaking of coffee, where's Troch?"

"Back by the cell, playing checkers with Orme." Merwine thought that would get a response from the retired sheriff, and it did. Not a verbal one, just the eyebrows went up.

"Got one more thing on my mind," and Charles Henry reached for his handkerchief again. "Seems like everybody I talk to is planning to be at this hanging." He eased back into the small chair and eyed Peter Merwine directly.

"They'll be 42 witnesses present," admitted Sheriff Merwine.

Sheriff Henry was so taken aback that he bolted up out of his chair, almost knocking it over. With his hands on his hips he stared at Sheriff Merwine in astonishment, his tone incredulous. "Good Holy

Jesus! Forty-two men and the gallows in an 18 by 18 foot cell? What the hell are you thinking, son?"

As an indulgent son addressing a father out-of-line, Peter Merwine smiled and calmly said, "Have a seat Sheriff."

Sheriff Henry did as he was told, his face flushed with concern, and embarrassment at his outburst.

"It's not like I'm selling tickets to this god-damn thing. The law requires a minimum number of witnesses; it doesn't say anything about a maximum." Peter Merwine continued, his voice low, his tone even. He had thought this over and wanted the old sheriff to know that. He reached into the middle drawer of his desk and took out a folded sheet of paper. "Here's a list of names. Most of these men have asked to be present. That's the complete list, I won't be adding to it."

Sheriff Henry took the paper and studied it for a moment. What he was checking for was understood. He handed the paper back and through the hint of a smile said, "Thank you, Sheriff." His name was at the top of the list.

Young Pete Merwine had matured quickly into the job of Sheriff of Monroe County. He stood up and offered his hand to Sheriff Henry, diplomatically indicating their meeting was over for today. He had learned that trick from Sheriff Henry.

TUESDAY, AUGUST 10, 1869

Bustle came to Stroudsburg with the sunrise. Merchants opened their shops and prepared for business. Horses and carriages filled the streets; pedestrians crowded the sidewalks in spite of the heat and dust and threat of a summer storm. The courthouse, banks, barber shops and taverns hummed like beehives. Through newspapers and posters, the inhabitants of the little town had been notified that on Wednesday, August 11, every shop would be closed, by order of Sheriff Merwine. The borough would be busy hanging Charlie Orme.

Valentine Kautz, master cabinet-maker and Bavarian immigrant, along with his best apprentice were inside the jail, painstakingly finishing the apparatus that would end a life. Several other journeymen carpenters were busy in the Ninth Street shop, hammering away at a coffin.

Breaking from their regular visiting schedule, both ministers arrived at the jail at 10a.m. and stayed with Charlie until noon, promising to return the next day at 10a.m. Typical of the mysteries of the human heart, close bonds are forged in trying times. Charlie felt a kinship with Rev. Ridgway from the Methodist Church in Stroudsburg, and the feeling was returned.

"Will you take this with you Reverend Ridgway?" Charlie offered a stack of papers, folded, dog-eared, and torn at the edges. "Wait till I'm gone, you know, dead, then read it. If you think these words can help some other poor soul, then use it, best way you can. And I thank you."

"I certainly will read it son. And I'll do as the good Lord directs me." Reverend Ridgway put his hand on Charlie's shoulder, and he and his fellow pastor, Reverend Pearce, turned and left the cell.

Together they walked in silence down Seventh Street, through the heat of the mid-day sun, until Reverend Pearce spoke. "Let's see what the little bastard wrote."

"The hell we will!" And Reverend Ridgway disappeared, manuscript held tight to his chest, into the throng of Main Street shoppers. He had given his word to a miserable sinner – and he would keep it.

Carrying a small cloth bag that held 24 round, wooden checker pieces in one hand and the heavy thick board in the other, Mr. Troch emerged from the cell area and walked past Sheriff Merwine, seated at his desk. The game was the personal property of Mr. Troch, kept at the jail only since he was given permission to play with Orme. He walked to the door, opened it slowly, then turned and spoke. "Wasn't no need to build that thing right in front of the boy." Sheriff Merwine rose in understanding, and Mr. Troch, clutching his beloved game, left the jail, his eyes wet.

WAITING FOR DEATH

Conflicting thoughts collided in the mind of Charles Orme as he waited for the death imposed on him by the State of Pennsylvania, County of Monroe, at an exact time, in a place certain.

It remained a riddle to him that he took a measure of comfort in the certainty of it. A pang of pity for those who stumble through their existence, never knowing the hour, place, or circumstance of their demise sat on his heart.

He came to terms with his regret of a wasted life; a life devoid of meaningful purpose.

He waited now, suspended in time and physically confined, the writing finished, the checker games concluded, the afternoon walks over.

He toyed with memories. Memories that took him beyond the walls of the Stroudsburg jail to times when he and Billy Brooks walked the land from Washington D.C., to the Pocono Plateau and their destiny. They took as they pleased, and put nothing back. He felt bad that his friend had died in their escape attempt, and shouldered some guilt for his death. Billy had been his only friend. Charlie did not know, and would never know, that Billy was half way across Ohio while he was only a few steps from the gallows. Degrees of heat and light passed through the bars of the tiny window on the back wall of the cell. The moon replaced the sun, the sun replaced the moon. Tuesday was pushed aside by an angry Wednesday, and Wednesday ushered in the execution of Charles Orme.

THE EXECUTION OF CHARLES ORME
WEDNESDAY, AUGUST 11, 1869

"It's 8 o'clock in the morning and it's already hot as hell." He took off his hat, fanned himself with it and leaned on the bridge railing.

"You sure are a fine observer of the weather, I do say," his friend countered, jokingly.

They were young men, just in their early twenties, born and raised in Stroudsburg, buddies all their lives. They worked together in the carpentry trade, and always had work. They were ambitious and never let an opportunity slip by. When Sheriff Merwine put out the word that men would be paid to direct traffic and keep order on the day of the hanging, they signed up.

They were each issued a badge and assigned to an area on lower Main Street, known locally as Five Points.

They had no idea what to expect, so as the traffic built and the town filled with countless hordes, they were surprised. Surprised not just by the number who came to town, but by their behavior.

"I swear, I ain't never seen so many people acting so crazy in my life. They're all giddy over a hangin'. And I do believe some of 'em is already drunk." He put his hat back on his head and adjusted the brim to deflect the glare of the mid-morning sun. His friend stood next to him in silence, also baffled by the merriment.

The commotion continued all morning and into the afternoon. The heat intensified as dust-choked revelers drank themselves silly.

One short step from the street, the somber jail alone separated these two opposing worlds, the cheerful from the cheerless.

At 9a.m. Mr. Troch took Charlie a breakfast of eggs and coffee. Orme said he had slept some during the night, but complained of a severe headache.

At 9:20a.m. a tub of hot, soapy water was brought to his heavily guarded cell where Orme bathed, then dressed in the black pants, white shirt, and black coat provided.

At 10a.m. Reverend Ridgway arrived, visibly upset by his walk through the throng of merrymakers. Not until he'd composed himself did he step into the cell and administer the sacraments to Orme, who was devout.

At 10:30a.m. Reverend Pearce arrived from Delaware Water Gap. He entered the cell, gushing an apology to Reverend Ridgway and Charles for his tardiness. Consideration for the condemned negated an explanation. All three knelt and prayed.

At 10:45a.m. the 42 selected witnesses trickled in and squeezed themselves into the 18 by 18 foot cell, adjacent to the smaller cell that had been Charlie's home for almost a year. Among these stood Sheriff Henry, Dr. Jackson, all 12 jurors and the men from the search teams. Family and close friends of Theodore Brodhead skirted the scaffold. Master-carpenter Valentine Kautz came to observe the workings of his device. One defense attorney, fresh from the ball field, shouldered his way to the back wall, farthest from the point of execution.

Elliot Kessler, notepad and pencil in hand, brazenly shoved his way through until he stood directly in front of the gallows. He was entitled to the best viewing area. The public depended on him to accurately report the details of Monroe County's first execution.

Mr. Troch sat in the jail office. He opened Charlie's Bible to the 23rd Psalm, then silently spoke the words from memory.

The cell grew unbearably hot. Without ventilation, the fetid odor of impending death filled the room. Faint raucous laughing and singing drifted into the jail. All inside burned with heat, some with shame.

At 10:55a.m. Sheriff Merwine led Charles Orme and the two ministers down the short hallway to the hanging cell. Then, the footfalls of Orme and Merwine scrapped along each stair step to the top of the gallows. Suddenly, from below, Reverend Ridgway blurted out, "Let's wait for the one o'clock train. There could be a pardon from the Governor in today's mail." Sheriff Merwine spun around and glared at the Reverend. From the scaffold platform Charles Orme spoke, directing his whisper to the Sheriff. "Will you grant me that? It is the last favor I will ask of you."

Two deputies ran to the station only to wait with young mail-carrier William Walton. At 1p.m. when the mail train arrived they ploughed through five mail bags for a letter from Governor Geary. A conscientious Quaker, Walton advised, "We must be quick, but thorough. If it's here and we miss it, we'll have to live with that the rest of our lives." He needn't have worried. The Governor had sent no pardon.

At 1:25p.m. they were back in the large cell and Sheriff Merwine, again, led Charles Orme up the steps of the gallows. He read the execution warrant, as stipulated by law, and then asked Orme if he had any last words. And of course, Charlie did. Whether to postpone the inevitable or at least to leave some doubt as to his guilt before his launch into eternity, Charlie began rambling.

He first stated that his trial had been unfair, then praised the work of his defense attorneys. He claimed Thomas Brodhead had misidentified him, then took responsibility for beating him senseless. He claimed mistreatment in the Stroudsburg jail, then thanked those at the jail who had been kind to him. He insisted, resolutely, that he had not murdered Theodore Brodhead. That part was true. He hadn't murdered Theodore Brodhead. Billy Brooks shot and killed Theodore Brodhead, but, then as now, the law found him equally guilty. He concluded, repeating that no man could say that he killed Theodore Brodhead. He turned and faced Sheriff Merwine, indicating he was finished.

At 1:45p.m. Sheriff Merwine bound Charlie's hands and legs with strips of rags and placed a piece of white cotton cloth over his head. He next took the noose, positioned it at Charlie's throat and pulled the knot tight against pale, clammy skin.

He turned to his deputy, positioned at the lever below, and signaled.

The deputy jerked back the lever. The trap door sprang open, and Charlie Orme fell through the opening, landing hard on the floor, the broken rope swinging back and forth above the scaffold platform.

From tight lips, gasps and oaths erupted. Men stared in disbelief.

First to react was Dr. Jackson. He lept forward and pulled Charlie up to a standing position. Dazed and choking, Charlie needed to be steadied; blood trickled into his right eye from a small cut on his forehead. Frustrated and angered over this botched procedure, Dr. Jackson shot Sheriff Merwine a look that said so, but he held his tongue.

Peter Merwine barked an order: two deputies scurried out of the cell and down the hall, quickly returning with a new rope ripped from a cot in a nearby cell.

Hastily retying the noose and throwing it over the top beam, Sheriff Merwine unceremoniously marched Charlie back up the steps. After looping the rope over Charlie's head, he again signaled for the drop to be opened. It was now 2p.m.

Charlie fell through but no distinctive, sharp crack of a neck breaking was heard. The rope held, but the knot began to slip. Charlie writhed and struggled against death. His body convulsed, then was still, then began to twitch and spasm again, then went limp. Two of the jurors vomited into their hands and the ambitious, young reporter fainted.

At 2:10p.m. Dr. Jackson stepped up to the dangling body and held his stethoscope to the center of Orme's chest. He heard a beating heart and anger and sympathy flooded his soul. He backed away and waited. Charlie spasmed and swung back and forth like a leaf caught in an afternoon breeze. He gasped, coughed, then went still.

At 2:15p.m. the doctor checked again and detected a faint heartbeat. Death by strangulation is a long, slow process. The twitching continued, off and on, for five more agonizing minutes.

At 2:20p.m. Dr. Jackson approached the body, held the stethoscope to the center of the chest but heard no sound. He peeled back an eyelid and tapped gently on the eye ball. No response.

At 2:21p.m., in a flat, emotionless voice, Dr. Jackson declared, "This man is dead."

In a not-so-calm but steady official voice, Sheriff Merwine ordered the cell to be cleared and the 42 witnesses made their way out of the Stroudsburg jail, shaken and bewildered.

The jail house bell was rung, signaling the execution's end, and those who worked at crowd control were now relieved of their duties. They gathered in front of the jail where the senior deputy handed them their stipends. The hotels and taverns reopened and the money quickly found its way back into the economic mainstream of Monroe County.

The town grew still and quiet, the energy of the gawking masses dissipated now in the late afternoon heat and dust.

By 4p.m. the lifeless body of Charles Orme lay loosely wrapped in a white sheet in the cell where he had met death. After dark, he was transported to the home and office of Dr. Jackson, and embalmed on Thursday, August 12.

THE BURIAL OF CHARLES ORME
FRIDAY – AUGUST 13, 1869

At day break on Friday, August 13, 1869 a small buggy, holding a coffin and pulled by two black horses, arrived at the corner of Eighth and Sarah Street. Four young deputies jumped from the vehicle and walked to the back of the home. Dr. Jackson ushered them into his make-shift morgue. After carrying the body of Charles Orme to the waiting coffin, they headed to the Stroudsburg Cemetery, waving to the good doctor as they departed.

By 10a.m., with dark, threatening rain clouds gathering in the mid-morning sky, they committed Charles Orme to the grave. No mourners attended, only the Sheriffs Merwine and Henry, four deputies and the Reverend Ridgway. The Reverend recited a few words after the last shovel of dirt landed on top of the mortal remains of young Charlie Orme, the man who had not murdered Theodore Brodhead.

"That's the end of it." Sheriff Merwine stated, "We need to get this damn thing behind us."

The group of seven left the unmarked grave and headed for town. Nobody wanted to get caught in the rain.

The Reverend had one more thing to do; he promised himself he'd do it Saturday. He always kept his promises, to the living and the dead.

THE LEGACY OF CHARLES ORME
SATURDAY, AUGUST 14, 1869

Reverend Ridgway sat alone in his study, looking out the window of the comfortable parsonage. The storm had passed and the heat and humidity of the afternoon prompted him to open all the windows and doors on the first floor. Though some pedestrian traffic cluttered Main Street and parishioners were entering and leaving his church, he determined he would not be disturbed until he finished the task he set for himself this afternoon. He slit open the envelope containing the pages Orme had given him and settled into his favorite chair. A gentle breeze carried the fragrance of wisteria into the room and relaxed him as he read Charlie's manuscript.

He noted the first page was dated July 13, 1869. The final entry, eight pages later, was marked August 10, 1869, one day before the execution. Punctuation and spelling indicated the boy had not been formally educated, but the handwriting was neat and legible. Though curious, he held no great expectations in regard to content. Expectation began to rise with the opening line: *"I write this in the hope that it may be the means of arresting the attention, and saving other young men from the path that leads to death and hell. The sacred volume declares "no drunkard shall inherit the kingdom of God."* Charlie now had a firm grip on the Reverend's attention. He read through it quickly, noting references to the Bible and the consequences of taking strong drink. Charlie warned about taking even one drink, and how lives are ruined and hearts are broken. He set himself as an example which led to the shameful death he now faced, always blaming his addiction to whiskey. On the last page, the final sentence read: *"I give you advice a good mother gave me – 'Keep out of bad company and don't drink.'"* Charlie rambled and repeated, but the Reverend loved it. He understood this would be a strong weapon. He would add it to his arsenal in the war for temperance.

The Reverend read through the pages again, more slowly and thoughtfully this time. The third time he read it, he began noting corrections on a separate sheet of paper. As the afternoon disappeared, the

Reverend was still intently studying Charlie's writing. He moved from his window seat to his desk. When his wife announced the evening meal was ready, he lovingly replied that he would eat later.

The sun retired to the western horizon and his wife retired to her bedroom and still the good Reverend worked at editing Charlie's letter. He made only minor changes in grammar, spelling and punctuation. He carefully retained the tone of a condemned man, calling out a warning from the edge of the grave.

He based his sermon that Sunday on the warning of those pages, and over the years the Monroe County Temperance Society printed and distributed many copies of those last words of Charles Orme. Charlie's plea, "Use it the best way you can," rang in the ears of Reverend Ridgway the rest of his life.

MID-JANUARY, 1900

William Walton left the Post Office at 3:30p.m. and trudged up Main Street, stepping over mounds of drifted snow. Turning right on Seventh Street, he was buffeted by an icy blast of winter wind. He held his hat with one hand and clutched a bulky, brown envelope in the other. Mid-way through the block, the empty lot at the corner Quaker Alley reminded him of the old jail where he, as a young carrier, had often delivered mail. He contemplated the passing of time: 25 years since that old jail had been torn down, and almost ten years since the new courthouse had been built. He quickened his pace, eager to get to the new jail and out of the cold.

He pulled the door open and entered, without knocking, to find young Sheriff Peter Merwine Jr. sitting behind his father's desk and three deputies gathered around the wood burning stove. He was greeted with familiarity.

"What brings the Post Master of our fine town out in this bitter cold?" asked the sheriff and son-of-a-sheriff. "Get yourself a cup of coffee."

"I'll get it for you, Bill," offered the oldest deputy. "I got to put some more wood in this stove 'fore it goes out." And he rose from his chair.

"Don't you boys have any criminals to catch?" William asked with a smile.

"Nope, caught 'em all yesterday," replied one of the younger deputies and they laughed the laugh of men who know each other well.

"Here's your coffee. One of you boys fetch our Post Master a chair."

"Thank you, and this is for you Sheriff. New mail carrier missed it this morning. Looks important so I thought I'd bring it up for you." William Walton, now seated in the chair by the desk, handed the brown envelope to Pete, Jr., who studied the face of it.

"Not addressed to me in particular. Just addressed to the Sheriff of Monroe County. Got a return address of McMurry, Washington. Can't get much further away than that." Sheriff Merwine Jr. turned the envelope over in his hands, thoughtfully studying it.

"Why don't you open it Sheriff? Might help ya find out what's inside." The stove tending deputy laughed and sat back down in his chair.

Pete Jr. slid two pieces of paper out of the envelope and looked, back and forth, from one to the other, several times. The others tried to read the expression on his face. Was he shocked, startled, mystified, baffled? The silence went on so long they became worried.

"What's it about, Sheriff?" A hint of concern had crept into the voice of the usually affable senior deputy.

"Back in '68, one of the Brodhead brothers was murdered. Theodore was his name. Happened over in the Gap. One of the murderers escaped and my Dad hung the other one, down in the old jail. I was pretty young at the time." Peter Merwine Jr. was speaking like a young man recalling a past he wasn't totally familiar with.

William Walton and the senior deputy exchanged puzzled looks. The two young deputies had no inkling of the event that had occurred before they were born.

The Post Master went first. "I was there, in the Gap. I went with one of the search teams, but I wasn't with the group that captured the murderers."

"Billy Brooks and Charlie Orme. The sons-a-bitches." The senior deputy wasn't smiling now; he was recalling, with bitterness, the terrible day, 32 years ago, when his friend and neighbor had been murdered. "It was my group that caught 'em. Had to save their ass from lynch mobs in the Gap and then again, here in town. Should have shot the bastards when I had the chance."

The sheriff looked up at his senior deputy and with a wry smile declared, "You may get a chance. This here letter says these lawmen out there in Washington have a man in jail who goes by the name Billy Brooks. They say he was bragging to a fellow ruffian that he killed a man in the Water Gap and escaped the hangman's noose. If we can give them a positive identification, they'll send him to us. Sent us a picture of the man." He handed the photograph to the senior deputy, and he and the post master studied it together.

William Walton inhaled audibly and said, "Good Heavens." It was the strongest oath the Quaker used.

"Holy shit," exclaimed the deputy, using one of his milder expressions. "That don't look nothing like the Billy Brooks I brought in here."

The Quaker and the Deputy continued to stare, in stunned silence at the picture. The years had not been kind to Billy Brooks, who, now in his mid-fifties looked like a man in his mid-eighties. Thirty plus years of hard living and heavy drinking had taken a toll on the young man who had cheated death and deprived citizens of Monroe County of justice.

"Sure would like to see Brooks hang, but I'm sworn to uphold the law, and I can't say for certain that's him." The deputy handed the picture back to the sheriff.

"Give me some names of men you think might recognize him." The sheriff addressed both older men while pulling a clean sheet of paper from his desk drawer.

Their shift over, having nothing to contribute and realizing they weren't included in this part of the conversation, the two young deputies stood up to leave.

"Throw some wood in the stove and clear the sidewalk before you guys go home."

"Yes Sheriff."

The senior deputy rose and refilled the coffee cups. "Not many of us left." He returned to his chair and closed his eyes, helping him see better in the dim light of distant memory. "Mr. Troch's gone, Sheriff Henry's gone. Summerfield Staples been dead for years. I'm the only one left of the five in the posse that captured 'em. It's been a long time."

"What about your Dad, Sheriff?" William Walton asked, his tone soft.

"I don't think so. Some days he doesn't even know who I am." Sorrow welled-up in his voice, but he stayed focused on the business at hand.

Walton continued, "They lived on a property in the Gap. I think a negro woman owned the land. Can't remember the name.

"Mrs. Huff. Her husband, Amos, was killed in the war. She moved away, years ago, don't know where." The deputy had a good memory and another idea. "Maybe them three attorneys what defended the two of 'em."

"That's good." Sheriff Merwine, Jr. scribbled on his paper. "I'll take this picture around to them tomorrow."

William Walton then offered, "After that, I can hang the picture in the post office." He was pleased with his idea. Both lawmen balked.

Not wanting to offend, young Sheriff Merwine smiled and said, "Thanks, but I want to think some more before I play that card." With a wisdom beyond his years and experience, he understood the ramifications of stirring up the public and producing a false identification. The flower of what would be best for the citizens of Monroe County blossomed in his heart and mind. He stood, indicating the session was over, a trick he learned from his father, and said, "Thank you, Gentlemen. Let's meet here a week from today to go over what we got."

The fading sun of a mid-winter day prompted him to light his desk lamp. He laid the letter and picture from the town of McMurry aside, picked up a report from the courthouse, but was unable to concentrate on it. The banality of his own bureaucratic paperwork was overcome by the importance of this identification request.

He picked up the picture again and stared at the man that, allegedly, murdered Theodore Brodhead. He envisioned himself visiting the lawyers and asking for identification. That's when a quick, sharp realization hit him. He didn't know who had defended Brooks and Orme. He had been a boy. He turned to the filing cabinets and started digging. Those drawers were stuffed with folders, new and old, some tied with string. Surely some newspaper article would name the defense attorneys.

It didn't take long. The filing system was orderly and, after all, there was only one murder file. He jotted down the names of three attorneys, glad that he recognized each name. Only one still maintained a law office on the square, but that did not concern him. He closed the old folder; a stray piece of paper floated to the floor; he knelt to retrieve it. Yellow and brittle, it had been cut from *The Jeffersonian*, a local paper. With a lawman's curiosity and care, he unfolded it on his desk to study it in the light. He first noticed the date in the margin, August, 1869. He saw it was a poem titled "Lament." Last, he noticed that the poet was his father. He was overcome with emotions he could not explain. He read quickly, quietly, absorbed by words and meaning.

LAMENT

By Sheriff Peter Merwine

Sad and gloomy was the town of Stroudsburg

the day Charles Orme was ordered out to die.

O where's the breast not dead to pity

but for him did many in this town heave a sigh.

He was brave and stood it nobly,

Farewell Charles, forever home,

He I see no more.

But his remains lie buried in the sumptuary

on the Pocono Creek's shore,

to try the realities of another world.

He could hear his heart pounding in his chest. He felt hot tears streaming down his face. He read it again, then again, then returned it to the file. He extinguished his lamp, locked the door and started walking home. The flower of action was now fully open in his mind. He would meet the attorneys, he would see the Post Master and the Senior Deputy next week. But in his heart he knew, "This is over. We gotta keep this damn thing behind us."

He entered his home and hung his heavy coat on the rack just inside the door. He stepped quickly to the blazing hearth. From deep in his well-cushioned chair and covered with a home-made quilt, the old sheriff smiled at his son, and nodded.

EPILOGUE

Other murders have occurred in Monroe County, but none ever enraged the citizens of Monroe County like this first murder.

Gone are the lynch mobs, gone is the clamor for immediate retribution.

We are either more civilized or more apathetic.

There is a village named 'Brodheadsville' and a waterway named 'Brodhead Creek', in Monroe County, but none of the individual players in this tragedy are remembered, although their actions deserve remembering.

ACKNOWLEDGMENTS

I owe a great deal to the following people who read the manuscript and offered their advice on content and style. Their input was invaluable to me and made the finished product the best it could be. Thank you very much: Sue Moore Jordan, Amy Leiser, Kelly Luciw, Ruth Reitenaur, Kathryn Ritter, Mark Abel and Martin Wilson.

I will always be very grateful for the research assistance of the following dedicated people who made this journey from idea to book enjoyable for me. The staff and volunteers at the Monroe County Historical Association are: Amy Leiser, Bret Fowler, Hope Kuchinski, Vicki Weaver, Agnes Webb, and Anda Staab. The archivist of Monroe County, B.J. Bachman, was a pleasure to work with and Martin and Sue Wilson from the Dutot Museum in Delaware Water Gap were wonderful to me. Mr. Rich Yukubowsky was very kind in providing me with information about the town of McMurry, Washington.

I counted heavily on my wife, Beverly, for help in so many areas but none more important than the support and encouragement she provided me with every day.

Finally, I want to acknowledge all the members of the Pocono Liars Club, who were always upbeat and generous with their praise.

BIBLIOGRAPHY

History of Monroe County, Pa. 1725 – 1976
A Bicentennial Project
John C. Appel - Coordinator

Pohoqualin – Delaware Water Gap Reflections
Francis R. Drake

History of the Bench and Bar of Monroe County
Hon. Arlington W. Williams

Monroe County, Pa. 175th Anniversary 1836 – 2011

"It Has Seamed Like War Today"
The Civil War letters of William D. Walton

"I am Giting Used to Solgering"
The Civil War letters of Lewis Long

Historic Easton – William J. Heller

The Stroudsburgs in the Poconos

Frank and Marie Summa – Patrice Summa Bair

Historic Trail of Stroudsburg – Richard R. Jackowski

The Jeffersonian – 12 August 1869

The Philadelphia Inquirer – 12 August 1869

The Stroudsburg Times – 26 February 1903

Monroe County Historical Association Library
The Brodhead Murder Part 1 and 11
Amy Leiser

Opinion of the Court:
Supreme Court, in and for the Eastern District of Pa.,
Hon. James Thompson, Chief Justice of Pa. Supreme Court.